FACING THE ENEMY

FACING THE ENEMY

HOW A NAZI YOUTH CAMP
IN AMERICA
TESTED A FRIENDSHIP

A NOVEL IN VERSE BY
BARBARA KRASNER

CALKINS CREEK
AN IMPRINT OF ASTRA BOOKS FOR YOUNG READERS
New York

For my Krasner ancestors who settled in
Newark, New Jersey, from Russia —BK

For information about permission to reproduce selections from this book,
please contact permissions@astrapublishinghouse.com.

Library of Congress Cataloging-in-Publication Data

Names: Krasner, Barbara, author.
Title: Facing the enemy : how a Nazi youth camp in america tested a
    friendship / Barbara Krasner.
Description: First edition. | New York : Calkins Creek, 2023. | Includes
    bibliographical references. | Summary: In 1930s Newark, NJ, best friends
    Tommy and Benny are torn apart when Tommy attends a Nazi youth camp for
    German Americans, and Benjy forms an anti-Nazi vigilante group.
Identifiers: LCCN 2022060063 (print) | LCCN 2022060064 (ebook) | ISBN
    9781662680250 (hardcover) | ISBN 9781662680267 (ebk)
Subjects: CYAC: Novels in verse. | Best friends--Fiction. |
    Friendship--Fiction. | Radicalism--Fiction. | Toleration--Fiction. |
    German Americans--Fiction. | Jews--United States--Fiction. | LCGFT:
    Novels in verse.
Classification: LCC PZ7.5.K74 Fac 2023 (print) | LCC PZ7.5.K74 (ebook) |
    DDC [Fic]--dc23
LC record available at https://lccn.loc.gov/2022060063
LC ebook record available at https://lccn.loc.gov/2022060064

Calkins Creek
An imprint of Astra Books for Young Readers, a division of Astra Publishing House
astrapublishinghouse.com
Printed in Canada

ISBN: 978-1-6626-8025-0 (hc)
ISBN: 978-1-6626-8026-7 (eBook)
Library of Congress Control Number: 2022060063

First edition

10 9 8 7 6 5 4 3 2 1

Design by Barbara Grzeslo
The text is set in Frutiger LT Std 45 Light.
The titles are set in Mader Regular.

CONTENTS

PART I:

FANFARE, 1937

INTRODUCING BENJY PUTERMAN

It's late spring, almost summer, 1937. Just four months and I can officially say I'm a freshman at Weequahic High. Rumors of a Nazi camp for kids opening in Sussex County somewhere are littering Newark streets like candy wrappers. My pop's a member of the Newark Minutemen, he and a bunch of other former prizefighters—they've been going around to meetings of these so-called Nazis in Newark, Irvington, and other parts of New Jersey and busting them up. The meetings and the people, I guess. Sometimes help comes from (shh!) gangsters like Longie Zwillman. But Longie's one of us, and he's been good to the Jews of Weequahic.

President Roosevelt is gearing up for a second term. His New Deal has been successful, from what I can see from my perch. He'll get us out of the Depression entirely. Hard to believe he took office just a couple of months after Herr Hitler (I've been taking German) took over Germany as Führer (leader) of the Third Reich (empire). He's gunning for an empire to last a thousand years. He's pals with Italy's dictator, Benito Mussolini. I think they're both nuts. At least Hitler and the Soviet Union's dictator, Josef Stalin, are sworn enemies. The papers say Hitler insists there will not be war, that no country wants war, and no country can afford war. I don't believe a word he says. After all, things are not going well for the Jews in Germany. A couple of years ago, Hitler put a decree in place to strip Jews of German citizenship. He dictated who Jews could marry and who they couldn't. They've lost their jobs. They're outcasts. Can't somebody do something about Herr Hitler?

Here in New Jersey and I guess elsewhere in the country is a new group who call themselves the German-American Bund. It's a club, a league. Pop tells me they used to be called the Friends of

New Germany until a congressman from New York, Sam Dickstein, shut them down. Rumor has it the Bund is behind this Nazi camp in New Jersey.

I know exactly how this summer will go. My best pal, Tommy Anspach, and I will sip sodas at Sol's while reading comics, play ball at Weequahic Park, and catch lightning bugs under the streetlights with mason jars. We'll celebrate our summer birthday (we'll both be fourteen on August 27!) in sleeping bags under the stars in my backyard. It'll be great—our last hurrah before we buckle down to a year of classes and homework in the number one high school in the state!

EXPECTATIONS

THOMAS ANSPACH
April 1937

Father no longer allows me to call him Vati.
Father no longer allows me to read comic books.
Father no longer allows me to be me.
Sometimes he calls me Rudi, the older brother
I didn't know, the one who died from scarlet fever
in Germany when paper money was so worthless
Mother used it as fuel to keep everyone warm.
But it didn't help Rudi or Germany,
and Mother and Father came to America
and had me.

I will never be their beloved Rudi.
I'm an American of German heritage.
Father sends me to learn German
in a special school on Saturdays.
He tells me I'm going to a special camp
to embrace my German heritage
as if I were growing up
in Germany itself. I will go to this camp.
I will prove to Father that Thomas
can be the son Rudi promised he would be.

FATHER TAKES ME TO A GERMAN-AMERICAN BUND MEETING

THOMAS

The head of the German-American league
stands on a platform in a belted shirt,
military-like. He speaks slowly, his eyes
peering, searing, leering
into mine. He says:

"To be and remain worthy of our Germanic blood,
our German Fatherland, and ancestral German blood

> That means he wants us Americans
> to remember we belong to Germany.

"Our German brothers and sisters fight for their existence, their
    honor
to cultivate our German language, customs, and ideals from shared
    blood

> That means we all have our German heritage
> in common. We need to come together.

"To stand up and be proud of all this,
to always remember in unity is strength, our blood."

> That means there's strength
> if we bond together.

Before I realize I'm doing it,
my arm is raised in salute and my voice
booms, *Sieg Heil.*

I NEVER KNEW
THOMAS

I never knew so many German-Americans lived
outside Newark. The people in this hall
have come from Irvington, that's right outside
Newark. But Haledon is near Paterson
and Paramus not far from there, Garfield too.

It is the first time I hear "Camp Nordland."
A new camp for kids like me with German parents
out in the New Jersey countryside, away
from the city. A place to bridge the old
and new, Germany with America.

As we stroll out of the meeting, Father
says, "Ru—Thomas, we're sending you
to Camp Nordland."
At least this time he only spoke
the first syllable of my dead
brother's name.

READ ALL ABOUT IT

THOMAS

Father thrusts his
German-American Bund
newspaper into my face.
"See here, this man
will be your camp director."
August Klapprott.
He looks
just like Fritz Kuhn, leader
of the Bund, holding
on to his leather holster across
his chest, fingers anchored
on his belt. Camp Nordland
opens on July 18. Just one
of many Bund camps across
the country to connect
American kids with our German
heritage. I wonder if that means
we'll get to drink the beer
that Father loves so much.

I WANT TO TELL BENJY, BUT FATHER STOPS ME
THOMAS

"Where do you think you're going?"
Father asks.

> "To tell Benjy all about Camp Nordland."
> (My hand is on the doorknob.)

"No, this you must not do."

> "Why not?"
> (I open the door.)

"The Putermans are Jewish."

> "I know."

"You can't be friends with
Benjy anymore."
(He stands and closes the door.)

"We don't concern ourselves
with Jewish people. You'll find
new friends, German friends,
at Nordland. Boys like yourself."

> "But, Benjy and I have been friends forever.
> We like to do the same things."

"Not anymore."

BECUSE
THOMAS
May 1937

Because you give me no choice
Because I like the special attention
Because I want to know more about where you came from
Father, I'll go to Nordland.

Because your eyes light up with pride
Because you write my name in shirts, shorts, and socks
Because I know you really want a cabin in the woods away from
     the city
Mother, I'll go to Nordland.

Because I'm now your only child
Because I'm all you have
Because I never want to disappoint you
Dear parents, Camp Nordland, here I come.

MALE CALL
THOMAS

"A letter for you," Mother says.
"It's from your new section leader
at Camp Nordland." It's addressed
to Thomas Anspach, not Tommy.
I open it. It's completely in German.

"I told you that you'll have
to speak German all the time
at camp," she says.

I roll my eyes. Slipped in
with the letter are the lyrics
to the German national anthem:

Deutschland, Deutschland über alles,
  Germany, Germany above all,
über alles in der Welt,
  above all else in the world,
wenn es stets zu Schutz and Trutze
  when always for protection and defense,
brüderlich zusammen hält,
  brothers stand together.

I am still singing the song to myself
as I fall asleep.

LET ME AT 'EM
BENJY

"Let me at 'em," Pop says
at the dinner table. That's what Mr. Nat Arno
said, Pop says, when they heard about
a Nazi club meeting in Irvington. Pop
is one of Mr. Arno's Minutemen. Just
the sound of that makes Pop stand up
straight, like he's a colonist fighting
against the British.

When Mr. Arno says, "Let me at 'em,"
he means business, Pop says. Mr. Arno
started boxing at fourteen,
his first match and first win at fifteen. His pop
didn't want him fighting so Mr. Arno
hitchhiked to Florida. Won a ton
of fights. Now, a bunch of years later,
he's back in Newark.
Jeez, even Newark's mayor, Meyer Ellenstein,
was a Jewish boxer, too.

So why the Minutemen? Why not the Boxers?
Pop's proud of his fights. He won't let
Mom touch the gold satin shorts
he wore in his last match. He gave up
boxing when I was born. But
he hasn't given up fighting—he just
doesn't use a ring anymore.

I'm going to box someday, too, just
like Benny Leonard, Newark's
most famous Jewish boxer.
I check my meager muscles
in the bathroom mirror. I have
a long way to go for anyone
to believe me when I say,
"Let me at 'em."

WHAT TOMMY WON'T BE DOING
BENJY
July 1, 1937

"I won't be playing ball with you
at Weequahic Park," Tommy says.

"I won't be hanging out after dinner with you
or having a Coke," Tommy says.

"I won't be opening up the fire hydrants
to cool us off," Tommy says.

"My parents have signed me up for camp
in the country. A lake, trees, fun," Tommy says.

"I'll talk to my parents so I can come, too!" I say.
"You can't come with me," Tommy says.
"No Jews allowed." He turns toward his house.
"And I'm Thomas now."

TOMMY DOESN'T NEED TO LEAVE NEWARK
BENJY

If Tommy wants to escape the city,
he could go, like we always do,
to Weequahic Park, throw a few balls around.

If Tommy wants to breathe fresh air
and the scent of grass, there's always my backyard,
narrow but deep.

Or the grassy median that divides Goldsmith Avenue
where we played hide-and-seek in the shrubs.

We've got a few trees, too, lining the curb,
next to the garbage cans.

It may not be Camp Nordland,
but it's home and it's ours.

A LESSON IN US CITIZENSHIP FROM MY FATHER
THOMAS

Citizenship *noun*: a way to cover up one's past in a foreign country. To be legally recognized as a new subject in a new country hides any evidence of wrongdoing or continued allegiance to the old country (in this case, Germany).

Naturalization *noun*: cements a person's loyalty to the new country, no matter how he really feels about the old country (in this case, Germany).

Allegiance *noun*: only to one's self.

An added bonus:
Remember that Fritz Kuhn is an intimate friend of Adolf Hitler.

A NEW DAY

THOMAS
July 18, 1937

Mother and Father squeeze our sedan
into one of the last parking spots. My parents
haven't stopped smiling since we left Newark.

We snake our way through the throng
to the Bund Hall. A path has been
made for the opening ceremony parade.

Girls in blue skirts and white blouses
strut down the center lane, faces
and posture disciplined, purposed.

Boys in brown shirts and ties
march up a grassy slope
playing tubas, trumpets, drums.

I am one of you, I want to shout.
I am selected among German-Americans
to attend Camp Nordland.

The swastika and eagle of Germany's Third Reich
flap alongside the Stars and Stripes,
although I've never before seen

the American flag hung vertically.
Director Klapprott takes his position
on the raised platform.

that is decorated with green garlands.
A radio speaker stands ready
to broadcast his words.

We begin a new day. I'm not one of them yet.
Next year, I'll be in the parade.
I am one of the chosen.

I FOR YOU AND YOU FOR ME

THOMAS

July 18, 1937

Mother and Father stand at attention
while Fritz Kuhn takes the podium,
his face red-hot with heat and purpose.
"We designed Camp Nordland to teach
the spirit of New Germany on this small
German piece of soil in America."

I've never been to Germany, not yet,
but Leader Kuhn says
the fields and forests
of Andover are just like Germany.

We're all brothers,
joined in song and racial ideals,
Leader Kuhn says, without Jews.
Without Benjy and the Putermans?
But before I can even think
about that, Father pokes me
to pay attention.

"I for you and you for me!"
Leader Kuhn says like a pledge, like
the Three Musketeers, "All
for one and one for all!"

It seems like he's talking only
to me. Like he wants only me
to hear his message. Like
I'm the only one who can

achieve his mission. You bridge
the gap, his face tells me,
between America and Germany.
His look is so intense I almost
take Father's hand.

Almost.

HOMAGE
THOMAS

This is a pageant
unlike any I've seen
before. A New Jersey
senator is here. So is the leader
of the Italian-American Blackshirts,
because Mussolini is a friend of Hitler.
Sorry, I meant the Führer, Herr Hitler.
The members
of the Italian group march
in solidarity.

My right elbow swings back,
my forearm lifts,
first to my shoulder,
then the elbow pushes
the entire arm into
the air until I feel
the muscles tighten
in my underarm.
I stretch out my arm:
Sieg Heil!
Sieg Heil!
Sieg Heil!

I glance at Father.
He is beaming.
He pats me on the back
before he raises his arm too.

THINGS YOU CAN FIND AT SOL'S LUNCHEONETTE
BENJY

The *Star-Ledger*
Newark Evening News
Baseball cards
Bazooka
Candy buttons, candy cigarettes
Baby Ruths, Sugar Daddy caramel pops
A sticky counter
Detective Comics, *Amazing Stories*,
Astounding Stories, and *Thrilling Wonder Stories*
Sticky menus with dabs of ketchup and mustard
Chipped plates with crimson rings
The best meatball sandwiches (sorry, Ma)
Old men with stale breath and yellowed teeth, jabbering in Yiddish
The pickle barrel
News about Nordland
The empty stool where Tommy used to sit.

THE MINUTEMEN MAKE PLANS
BENJY
July 19, 1937

Pop says the Minutemen are gathering,
making plans—joining forces with Longie Zwillman's
Third Ward gangsters—to bring down the camp.

I want to be a part of it.
Let me at 'em, too.
They stole my best friend.

THE EAGLE SOARS
THOMAS

My heart soars over the pines
like a hawk—no, an *eagle,*
like the one in the Reich emblem.

Bund leader Kuhn inspires us
with words of unity, of Germany, of greatness,
the wise owl who sees our future.

The light beyond the clearing
reflects like a mirror on the lake
behind him. Our voices,

stars of light, glide past the howls
of naysayers. Our voices rise up
over the hills as Germany rises up
to claim what is ours.

Deutschland über Alles.

THE STAR OF DAVID
BENJY

My skin is Jewish, there's nothing I can do,
can't change my name or hide my circumcision
or Ma's Star of David, that heirloom and tattoo.

I can't change my Hebrew name to something new,
can't move the mezuzah without superstition.
My skin is Jewish, there's nothing I can do.

A lot of us Jews live here on Goldsmith Avenue,
a lot of Germans, too, since before Prohibition.
But Ma still wears that Star of David, that heirloom, that tattoo.

Hebes, the Germans call us as they spew.
We call them Krauts with derision.
My skin is Jewish, there's nothing I can do.

Till now we've lived peacefully, tension's overdue.
Now the Bund boils up antisemitism.
Hide that Star of David, that heirloom, that tattoo.

Tommy's off to Camp Nordland for six weeks with mountain view.
He doesn't wave goodbye, gives no recognition.
He only sees my skin is Jewish, there's nothing I can do.

Tommy wears his brown shirt and shorts, spit-polished shoes.
I hear him speak German with great precision.
My skin is Jewish, there's nothing I can do.
Into it burns that Star of David, that heirloom, my tattoo.

GERMANIZATION
THOMAS

If I could repaint my room,
I'd paint it Homeland Red
with Aryan White and Swastika Black accents.
Maybe I'd suggest Rhine River Brown or Mosel Blue
to my parents for their room. Or Lederhosen Leather
or Dirndl Green? We could buy a Teutonic tapestry
for the front parlor and paintings that mimic the masters
like Hans Holbein the Younger. We'd import our appliances
from Germany, have a *Willkommen* mat on our front stoop.
My mother would fill the fireplace mantel with Hummel figurines
and Father would flesh out his pipe and beer stein collection.
Every year we'd make a pilgrimage to the Fatherland,
hike the German mountains, fill our nostrils
with edelweiss, and congratulate each other
on our German blood after a meal of sauerbraten and wurst.

SPINNING THE COLORS
BENJY
July 1937

"And remember to clean your room,"
Ma yells from the kitchen. I climb the stairs
and I know I should put my clothes away
that Ma's just pulled off the line in the backyard.
But I pull out the kaleidoscope Tommy and I
used to play with. He would get all technical
and explain how the stuff inside is angled for reflection.

I just liked the colors and the patterns. But it's interesting
that I could see a butterfly's wings and Tommy
could see an explosion. Were we looking
at the same thing?

I wondered then if we lived in two
different worlds.
Now I know we do.

IN EXCHANGE
THOMAS

One of the fellows in my bunk
hands me a leaflet from Germany.
He is from Germany. "I am
an exchange student," he says
in German, of course.
Does that mean an American kid
has gone to Germany as part
of the exchange? I'm not going
to tell Father or else he'll volunteer
me to go. "There are
lots of us," he says, "hundreds."
He opens a pack of German cookies,
crumbs falling onto the ground.
Hundreds of kids, hundreds of crumbs.
No one cleans them up.

WE'VE GOT NAZIS, ALL RIGHT

BENJY

I come home from Sol's
and Mr. Arno is sitting
at our kitchen table
having a snack of Grandma's
latest noodle pudding. Pop
says, "That can't be right.
Nat, you're saying hundreds
of German kids
are coming here, posing
as exchange students?"

Mr. Arno says, "They're not here to study,
that's for sure. They're here to
spread lies. You know about
Camp Nordland?"

"Tommy goes there," I throw the words
like a right hook. I dig my own fork
into Grandma's pudding. It's not the kind
you eat with a spoon like the chocolate
pudding Mom makes from a box.

"Well, kid, if your pal goes to Nordland,"
Mr. Arno continues, "he's speaking German—
and only German. All the time."

Pop leans into the table.
"And that's why all these organizations,
even Congress, are calling for an investigation?"

Mr. Arno takes another bite
and pushes the plate away.
"Yup. We've got Nazis, all right,
right here in Jersey. Right here in Newark,
and definitely in Andover."

I push away my plate now too. The noodles
begin to look like battalions of soldiers.
Nazis in Andover.
Tommy's in Andover.

THE NEW PRISTINE ROUTINE
THOMAS

The bugle blasts reveille at 6:30 a.m.,
we have 35 minutes to rush to the showers,
iron our clothes, polish our shoes.
Another 25 minutes to make our beds,
clean our barracks till they're pristine.
Inspection takes 10 minutes and then
roll call, rewarded by breakfast.
We get our chores out of the way
until the day heats up and we
have our morning swim in the lake.
No rest after lunch! We sing!
Muster our energy for the javelin throw
and the archery field. Afternoon swim
in the lake. After dinner we gather round
to sing yet again, our pristine voices
reaching our cousins in Germany.
We come together each night at 7:30
for evening lectures, then lights out
with taps at 9:30. A day well spent,
pristine health and vigor.
We are one, we German-American youth
of New Jersey! I for you and you for me!

We are the future carriers of New Germany's
ideals in America. *Sieg Heil!*

MORNING EXERCISES
THOMAS

The beat of our feet
hitting the gravel
as wooden sticks hit the skin
of the drum.
The beat of our feet
as we round the camp's main building,
building momentum
left, right.
Right is our might,
the group Führer reminds
us with each
beat of our feet
on concrete
left, right.
We march morn till night
in tight lines
of matching, muscled limbs.
We march
We march
knees locked,
lock step.
Hundreds of feet
hit the beat
left, right
left, right.
We're in a grove,
we hit the groove,
sole by sole.
Sticks hit drums
belted across the body,

lightning fringed-flags unfurl,
billow to trumpet shrill.
Stars and stripes up
the flagpole, flanked
by lightning bolt
and swastika.

I USED TO SPELL FUN T-O-M-M-Y
BENJY

No trips downtown
No tossing a ball around in the park.
Where has fun gone without Tommy?

No *Amazing* or *Astounding Stories*
No *Detective Comics.*
Where has fun gone without Tommy?

No playing pranks on the neighbors
No belly laughs at knock-knock jokes.
It's just no fun without Tommy.

WHAT HELPS US SLEEP AT NIGHT
THOMAS

Orange swirling flame of days
as the sun sets over the Andover hills.

A good day's worth of tilling the land,
sweat well earned on tightened bodies.

Hands clutch wheelbarrow handles by day,
hands press imaginary rifle triggers by night.

NO PARTY MOOD
THOMAS
July 25, 1937

It's my second weekend
at Nordland. Mother and Father
have rented a cabin.

We march
We salute
Music, violins mostly, pipes in through
the loudspeakers.

Father pulls Mother
up to the dance floor
of the beer hall.
I've never seen him
do the waltz before.
He moves as if he's been
dancing his whole life.
Mother practically
squeals in delight
as he twirls her
around the floor.

But then in the corner
newspapermen wait
in no party mood
for Camp Nordland's
Director Klapprott,
in the beer hall. Their
fingers tap on the wooden
tables.

I snake my way over.
I want to know what
they're saying.
One reporter in a fedora asks,
"The American Legion
and the Veterans of Foreign Wars
want an FBI investigation of
Camp Nordland.
Any comment?"

Cool as a movie theater
on a hot day, Director Klapprott
smiles. He says, "I welcome it.
"We've done nothing wrong."

IN THE BEER HALL AT NORDLAND
THOMAS

Wooden clock cuckoos in the beer hall.
Empty beer steins from Munich sit on the shelves,
    waiting for weekending adults.
Der Führer of Germany, Adolf Hitler, looks down from paneled walls
while leader of the German-American Bund, Fritz Kuhn, looks up
    to him.
The open sky above the trees offers endless possibilities.

WE'RE GOING TO TAKE A LITTLE RIDE
BENJY
July 26, 1937

"We're going to take a little ride,"
Mr. Arno says as he puts his
dish in the sink. Mom smiles.

"We're going to visit this
Camp Nordland—me
and the other Minutemen."

"Got a map of New Jersey?"
he asks. Pop goes into
the living room and pulls
out a Triple-A map, unfolds
it over the kitchen table.
"Yup, there!"
Mr. Arno points to an area
northwest of Newark.

"An ammunition
plant?" Pop asks.

"Very strategic, these Bund
guys, putting their new camp
near a powder keg.
Sabotage
is on their minds, boys.
Sabotage."

Pop folds up the map the way
only an adult can. "We're going
to take a little ride to Andover,"
he says.

I fall asleep with the name
Andover stamped on the map
in my mind, the line to it so clear.

BIG MOUTH
BENJY
July 29, 1937

They say Sam Dickstein,
a Democratic rep for New York,
has a big mouth. He's raising a ruckus.
He names names.
Lots of German names, names of Nazis
in New York and New Jersey, names of neighbors
and shopkeepers who work behind closed doors
against us Jews.
With that big mouth he'll KO
the German-American Bund
that rose from the ashes
of the Friends of New Germany.
He put the kibosh on them when
I was in grade school. Pop told
me, all you need is a big mouth,
a platform in Congress,
and a reporter.

HOW NOW, BLACK COW
BENJY

Tommy drinks the black milk of fascism
while I drink Hershey's chocolate syrup in milk.

Tommy drinks the black milk of lies and propaganda
while I beat on the drum of democracy.

Tommy drinks the black milk of the crooked cross
while I swarm with Newark's Minutemen.

Before long, Tommy's tongue and teeth will turn black
while mine remain red, white, and blue.

AN ANNOUNCEMENT
THOMAS

The youth leader stands before us,
a yardstick in salute,
hand raised to the forehead,
chest raised in perpetual inhale.

"We observe four holidays:
February 22—George Washington's Birthday
April 20—Führer Adolf Hitler's Birthday
July 4—America's Independence Day
October 6—German Day

"German Day commemorates
the founding of Germantown,
Pennsylvania. The first German
foothold in America."

Huzzah!

IF I WERE ELECTED
BENJY

My fellow Congressmen and especially
you, Representative Dickstein:

Let me tell you about Camp Nordland.
It is a hotbed of Nazis.
Yes, Nazis.
They pull my friend Tommy's
German heritage and stuff it
into a poisoned arrow. They train him
to fling hatred from a bent bow of gobbledy-gook.

Let's shut down this camp, I say.
Let's expose it for what it is.
Are you with me?

WHO'S RIGHT, WHO'S WRONG?
BENJY AND THOMAS
August 5, 1937

Dickstein's big stick is making headway

                         Dickstein's nuts

He's named twelve more Nazi
agitators.

                    Dickstein made up this so-called list
                          of Nazi leaders in America

Named them
Blamed them
Flamed them

                         Dickstein names people
                             who are dead

Better send those passports
packing! The Feds will deport
you home to the Fatherland.

                  Director Klapprott says only 10 percent
                      of the people Dickstein names
                                are Bund members.
                                   He would know.

REPEAT PERFORMANCE
BENJY

Again and again my fists join
the prizewinning pugilist posse
of the Newark Minutemen who will
pummel the jaw and maw of the Bund
until again and again their toothless words
spew lifeless to the ground to be ground
by our feet. Again and again Nat Arno
will raid their meetings, lead a black sedan
caravan to Nordland, even though
again and again someone tips off the police
and the camp director knows we're coming
for him.

REFLECTIONS
THOMAS

In the rocks, I see an ancient Teutonic warrior,
spine proud, jaw determined, headdress
ready for battle.

In the lake, I see a pathway
through a scrim to the mountains
from this New Jersey immigrant melting pot
to the pure empire we create together.

In the clouds, no, not clouds,
snow-covered Alps I've not yet seen
but will hike one day
as a member of the Reich
and there I will find
a rock with the face of an ancient warrior.
My face.

SEWING BASKET
BENJY

Ma's sewing basket holds spools of thread
wound boxer-fist tight. The white thread barely covers
the spool's wood. Ma uses it to mend my torn shirt pockets,
and darn Pop's shirt sleeves at the elbows.

Ma's sewing basket holds needles
to guide the thread. Ma squints to thread the narrow eye,
she licks the ends of the thread. A needle darts in and out
of fabric to make separate pieces stick together.

Ma's sewing basket holds a pockmarked metal thimble
to protect her finger while she sews,
a shield she dons because she knows the danger ahead
in bringing two sides together.

Ma's sewing basket holds papers of straight pins,
metal daggers to hold things in place: hems, collars, zippers.
Pull them out, and they leave vampire-like holes
if you know where to look.

Ma's sewing basket holds tailor's chalk,
squares of blue or white or pink to mark
where to take something in or let it out.
Brush the dust away; it leaves no mark.

But there's nothing in Ma's sewing basket
No thread strong enough
No needle big enough
No thimble large enough
No pins piercing enough
No chalk sturdy enough
That can stitch Tommy and me back together.

FAILURE IS NOT AN OPTION
THOMAS

Fear creeps into our tents
and scurries into floorboard spaces
between pillow and pillowcase,
between bristles of toothbrush and teeth of comb.

Fear grips my hands during drills.
What if I turn left instead of right?
What if I fall out of formation instead of
      standing at ease?
What if I halt instead of continuing
      to march?
What if my socks slide into my shoes?
Fear drips down my face like sunstroke.

I have to rid myself of it, quell my flinches.
I have to fear nothing
feel nothing
become nothing
so I can be something,
someone respected.

ONE WORD
THOMAS

One little word, that's all I want
One little word won't break the bank
One little word won't cause any harm
One little word Father can say to me
     When I win a javelin throw
     When I win a relay race
     When I win Director Klapprott's favor
One little word—
Good!—
is all I want.

ROOKIES AT LIFE
BENJY

All Tommy must do is train
in the rain, train in the sun,
train day and night, carrying his gear
like a wedding gown train. I'd rather
he take the train to Newark
if there is even a train where he is
and come back home and join
me at Weequahic Park, because
we could seriously train for
one of Weequahic High's sports teams
next year. Is he still thinking about
college or does he want to now train
for a trade like his father and be a plumber?

IN THE JUNIOR ARMY
THOMAS

Crates of Campbell's Pork & Beans
Prunes from Santa Clara
Icy Point salmon
We're in the junior army

Drills in high grass
Run, drop, crawl
With elbows and knees
We're in the junior army

Use that shovel to dig a ditch
Use that scythe to clear the land
Use that pickax to break through rocks
Use that salute to show you're loyal

THE DRIFTERS
BENJY

At the eighth-grade farewell dance,
Tommy and I sat on the couch
outside the dance hall the school
had rented. Everyone else was slow dancing,
one couple was even necking
until the principal and the dean of students
broke them apart.

Tommy and I didn't care about any of this.
Sure, I had hoped to dance, to muster
enough courage to ask Lilly Klein to the floor.
There I was in my new blue jacket,
Pop's old blue-striped shirt and light
brown trousers. Tommy didn't even
bother with a jacket and almost wasn't let
into the dance. We sat on that sofa,
me with my hands folded between my knees,
Tommy with his arms crossed, talking
about how Weequahic High was going
to be different. I was afraid that with
so many more people, we'd drift apart.

Lordy, we had no idea just how far we'd drift.

MORNING SONG
BENJY AND THOMAS

I wake up to rumbling garbage trucks
on cobblestone. Must be a Tuesday.

I wake up, owls hoot
farewell in the morning dark. Orange juice awaits.

It's going to be sizzling today
and the morning sun beats
through the kitchen windows.

I breathe in crisp air,
goose bumps on my arms and legs.
Good morning, Nordland, the trumpet sounds
in reveille.

Neighborhood dogs bark out
a rhythmic syncopation
worthy of Benny Goodman.

THE ALL AND ALWAYS CREED
THOMAS

We march all day, we march all night.
Bratwurst, Weisswurst is all we bite.
We turn away from the left, always veer to the right,
our formations always carefully structured and tight.
One day for Hitler we'll go to fight
and lines from his book, *My Struggle*, we'll cite.
He fills our heritage with voracious appetite
to claim what's ours, our primal birthright.
We train to smite the Israelites.
I push away thoughts of Benjy, a Semite,
and them, those termites, we must indict
to a fate only Hitler's imagined, might for right.

STOWAWAY

BENJY
August 8, 1937

I squeeze into the eighth and last Minutemen car
at the corner of Prince Street and Springfield Ave.
It's nine o'clock. I stay out of Pop's and Mr. Arno's
line of sight. I'm a stowaway who didn't eat
breakfast. My stomach rumbles.

It's an attack, I heard last night. Vigilantes
without weapons. Our tires crunch on dry grass
at the camp around noon. My stomach grumbles.

The campground is a wall of people—
and policemen. "They knew we were coming,"
someone whispers. No swastikas, no Nazi flags,
no uniforms. Instead, banners proclaim
Youth Sports Day.

I spot Tommy in a tee and shorts, stretching back
his elbow to catapult an arrow into a target.
Bull's-eye. My stomach crumbles.

METAMORPHOSIS
BENJY

I see him, Tommy,
hand in the air flinging
the javelin aimed
at an unknown enemy.

All the boys wear
white sleeveless undershirts,
shorts, bravado. They
are bumblebees
ready to suck nectar,
ready to sting.

Nestled next to canteens,
a squadron of rifles.
Cock, shoot.
Ready, aim.
Ain't this great fun.

Sunflowered
blades of grass
shield me from impaling
Dracula stakes. Spears
thrown by campers
like Berlin Olympians.

Tommy's laughing.
Tommy's speaking German.
His transformation is complete:
Like Boris Karloff, he's
been Frankenstein'd
Now he's Thomas,
the Teutonic knight.

CHRYSALIS
THOMAS

We don't pray to lay ourselves down to sleep
Our bodies are spent, welcome restful sleep

Javelin, archery, swimming each day
We relax on cool sheets, lulled to sleep

The anthem reverberates in our ears
It calls in Wagner's Siegfried, "Go to sleep!"

No Valkyries can touch or harm us,
the Reich-protected, in swastika'd sleep

The eagle's wings enfold us, bring us near
We close our eyes, moonful nights, stars of sleep

Thomas, you did not live like this before
Rise from your chrysalis, rise from your sleep!

I HAVE A VISION
BENJY

"When can we go again, Pop?" I ask
on the way home from Nordland.

Pop tussles my hair. "Not you,
young pup. Leave it to the Minutemen."

But in my head I see me leading
a group of kids to the campgrounds.
I see us raising a ruckus, causing
a police-worthy disturbance,
so when we go running past
the guards, the police aren't far
behind us. We
punch to the gut!
Uppercut to the chin!
Pound the breadbasket!

"Promise me, Benjy," Pop says,
as we climb the front stairs
to our house, "promise me
you won't go on your own."

I nod, knowing he can't see
my fingers crossed behind me.

A KNIFE'S MULTIPLE PURPOSES
THOMAS

I carry the knife in my belt,
always prepared
to slice a knot,
sever a tie,
clip an attitude.

We all wear the knives
to trim our fears,
mince a contrary thought,
snip a snide remark:

>Go back where you came from!
>We don't want Germans in America!
>Didn't you learn anything in the Great War?
>Anyone who follows Hitler follows blindly.

The knife reminds us
of the line from the song,
"When Jewish blood spurts
from the knife." I try not
to think of Benjy. I try not
to think of anyone I know.

The knife doesn't care
who gets hurt.

SHINE THE LIGHT
BENJY AND THOMAS

It is Friday and Ma prepares
for the Sabbath, candlesticks
gleaming in the setting sunlight
filtered through the kitchen window.
Ma will light the candles soon
in her weekly ritual and prayer.

It is Friday night and Mother prepares
for a weekend at the rented cabin
at Camp Nordland. Two days and nights
of German brotherhood, song, swimming,
and for Father, drinking.
He loves his beer—the darker, the better.

The lights cast a glow
over the darkened room
as Pop goes to shul
to hang out with the men,
and pray, of course.
Ma has her bean stew on the stovetop,
set low. Traditions forbid cooking
on the Sabbath.

The lights cast a glow outside the camp's
main building and we use flashlights to find our cabin.
"This reminds me of camp in the mountains,"

Father says, leading the way, carrying our bundles.
Mother's made a plum cake
and a *schnitzel* with *spaetzle* noodles.

It's Friday night and I wonder
what Tommy is doing.

It's Friday night and I push
thoughts of Benjy out of my head.

PURIFICATION
THOMAS

The tent fills with the scent of nature
and Ivory Soap 99.44% pure.
Somewhere in the distance an owl hoots.
No one stirs. I slip into my cot's starched
white top sheet, pull out my flashlight
and pick up where I left off in
Hitler's *Mein Kampf, My Struggle*.
Somewhere in the distance an owl hoots.

YEAR-ROUND CAMPING
THOMAS

Nordland is more than a summer camp
Nordland is open throughout the year
    Holidays
    Celebrations
    Rallies
Nordland is a constant for New Jersey Germans
Nordland finds occasions for us to gather in solidarity

IT'S MY BIRTHDAY
BENJY AND THOMAS
August 27, 1937

Ma buys a cake from the local bakery
and sticks in a 1 and a 4. It's official!
I'm fourteen.

> Mother bakes a cake from scratch
> but doesn't let me lick the spoon of batter
> or chocolate frosting.
> She says, "You're too old for that. You're fourteen!"

Pop turns off the lights
and Ma delivers the cake
to the table, candles burning.
They sing, "Happy birthday to you!"

> Mother brings the cake to the table
> and Father sings "Hoch sollst du leben,"
> the traditional German birthday song,
> "Long Shall You Live."

What Pop and Ma lack in their singing
abilities, they make up for with a stack
of comic books and a new suit
to wear for my first day at Weequahic High.

> Father's tenor rings out and I think about
> how he might have sung out for Rudi.
> Wishing Rudi a long life didn't make it so.
> Father and Mother give me
> a briefcase for my first day at Weequahic High.

A MIRAGE
BENJY
September 7, 1937

Summer's over. We're back in school.
Tommy! Tommy! Over here!

He doesn't look up. His hair looks blonder,
His eyes bluer. "Dirty Jew!"

Weequahic High is the last place he'd
want to say that. He'll get clobbered!

At Weequahic High, Jews are the majority!

I wish I could erase the whole summer,
be back in 1936 when we played ball

at the park, caught lightning bugs
in mason jars, ate watermelon slices,

trying to see who could spit the seeds the farthest.
"Tommy! Tommy! Over here!"

THE GREATEST DISTANCE BETWEEN TWO POINTS
THOMAS

Remote is the feeling when I see Benjy
in the hallway but have to stop
myself from saying hi.

Remote is the feeling on Saturday afternoons
when I can't go over to his house
or swivel with him on the stools at Sol's.

Remote is the feeling on the fields
at Nordland when I'd rather hit a home run
and round the bases at Weequahic Park.

Remote grows the distance between me and Father's
demands I find German friends. Remote grows
the distance between Father's sober moments.

CAN YOU STAND UP WHILE SITTING DOWN?
BENJY
September 10, 1937

"You should have seen them all,"
Pop says at the dinner table,
waiting for Ma to ladle out
the borscht—pink soup with sour cream
and a boiled potato.
I'd rather have a hamburger.
"Dozens of Great War veterans—
The American Legion
Veterans of Foreign Wars
Jewish War Vets
Irish Vets
even guys with Purple Hearts. All
to fight against Nazis in New Jersey,
in America."

"Did you say anything at the meeting,
Pop?" I ask. Of course, he did.
He's a stand-up guy. I could just
see him, waiting, just waiting
for the right moment—
Down with the Nazis
Down with the Bund
Down with hatred
We demand an investigation.

But all he says is, "I'm not
a veteran, young pup. I haven't fought
in a war like these guys. I haven't
served my country. It wasn't my place

to speak up. We Minutemen
were there for protection."

I roll the potato in my borscht,
mash it up and try not to think
of Pepto Bismol, although right now
it might ease the way my stomach feels.

THE FIRST SPAR
THOMAS AND BENJY

I don't need your help.

                                        He's pretending.

Stay away from me.

                                        He's hiding.

We're not friends anymore.

                                        He's lying.

You're just a dirty Jew, vermin.
Crawl back under the rock
where you belong.

                              That's not even Tommy talking.

THE THINGS I CARRY, MY YOM KIPPUR THINKING

BENJY
September 15, 1937

I carry the brick and mortar of ancient slaves in Egypt
I carry the lies that matzoh is made from blood of Christian children
I carry the fear of persecution, the burden of my ancestors
I carry the joy of tradition and an ancient, shared language.
The Jews of Germany whisper the same prayers
as the Jews of Weequahic. When we say Yizkor,
we want G-d to remember those who came before us.
We pledge our charity in the name of our lost loved ones.

THE CLOSING FESTIVAL
THOMAS
September 16, 1937

Leader Kuhn stands at the podium
to celebrate the closing of Nordland's
first season.

Huzzah!
Huzzah!
Huzzah!

Eighteen thousand people
squish into corners, dirt,
and blades of grass that have
seen brighter days of summer.

Leader Kuhn says, "Samuel Dickstein,
come up here and see our camp,
talk to us." The crowd roars.

Sieg heil!
Sieg heil!
Sieg heil!

The joke's on Dickstein,
Leader Kuhn says. He's made
Nordland more famous
than any of us could dream!

Leader Kuhn says to us all
that the Bund needs our
contributions to add to
Nordland's buildings. He says

we should give "that 40 cents
which you spend
in a Jewish movie house."

We goose-step along the path
by the beer hall, arms outstretched
under the protection of
three American flags
and one swastika banner.

I'm still thinking about Dickstein
with every step.
Dick-stein
Dick-stein
Dick-stein
as if we could stomp
out his name,
his Jewish name.

WAKE UP!
BENJY

I want to wake you up, old friend
to let you know your brain is mush.
Camp Nordland has made your mind bend.

The games, the songs, they never end,
the Reich, new Germany, they gush.
I want to wake you up, old friend.

I saw you that day, arrow's end,
surrounded by forest so lush.
Camp Nordland has made your mind bend.

You've treated me with hate, your trend.
Your words spit fire, spewed vile slush.
I want to make you up, old friend.

Why did your dad make you attend?
Force you to change, old friendships crush?
Camp Nordland has made your mind bend.

And you, my Tommy, can you mend?
Can you move past the lies? Now? Rush!
I want to wake you up, old friend.
Camp Nordland has made your mind bend.

A LETTER TO THOMAS
BENJY

My words bounce off your armor
but I know that armor is just tinfoil
that can crumble and tear.
So I'll keep asking the words
in the same formation, combination
until you remove your mask
and show me the Tommy you used to be.

You've forgotten who you are
You've forgotten where you are
You've forgotten who I am
You listen to crackpots and lightning-cracking
       emblems and slurs.

You came to me when you failed the spelling test
in third grade and you were afraid to go home.
You came to me when your father got drunk
and smacked you into the kitchen cabinets.
You came to me when your Oma died
and you thought it was your fault for forgetting
to close the front door.
I'm going to pin this note to your jacket
the way your mother used to pin your mittens.
Read it!
And then see if you can tell me
with a clear conscience
I'm vermin like all Jews.

INFILTRATION
BENJY

Mr. Zucker is up at his desk
teaching us new German vocabulary.
Suddenly Mr. Zucker, a Newark Jew, grows
a toothbrush mustache like Adolf Hitler
and goes into hysterics,
speeding up his voice to crescendo.
I shake my head to bring myself back to reality
and lean back into the chair connected to my desk,
taking small comfort
that Mr. Zucker has a trace of a Yiddish
accent in his German.

THE SPLIT
BENJY

It's been a long time since Tommy and I
split a banana split at Sol's. A mound of banana halves,
three scoops of ice cream—vanilla, chocolate, and pistachio—
chocolate sauce, marshmallow sauce, caramel,
chopped peanuts, whipped cream, and a maraschino
cherry. But now that Tommy's split
for Camp Nordland, splitting his time
between Weequahic High and special events
held at the camp, I don't run into him often
at school outside of German class. I stare at him
in class, stare him down like I can telepathically
command him to some action. It doesn't work.
I'd like to split open his brain and see the bunk
he's been noodling on there. And just once
I'd like him to make a mistake in German class.
Even Tommy is still human,
I think.

OPPOSING CONTENDERS
BENJY

The chasm between us widens, fills with withering
blades of grass and crumpled leaves.

Tommy and I move about our day silently
through the hallways. I watch him descend
into the darkness of lonely stairwells.

Uncertain of his certainty, he thinks
he knows his Teutonic future. Not even
the fortune teller downtown on Halsey Street
knows what's in store for any of us.

Now we're both held by the ropes
of opposite corners of the boxing ring.
He'll spew his clichés at me. But my
pugilistic power and fancy footwork
will first confuse and then clobber him.

WHEN THERE'S NO BOXING RING
BENJY

Pop sits at the table, arms folded,
looking like he wishes dinner is brisket
instead of a scrawny chicken
from the poultry market
downtown on Prince Street.

Ma flits between us,
serving first the chicken soup
with kneidlach and then eggs and onions
with shmaltz. If Zayde
were still alive, he'd say, "Oy, I can
feel my arteries hardening already,"
and they did. Heart attack.

By the time the pieces still clinging
to the chicken carcass are saved for tomorrow,
Pop's unfolds his appetite for a fight
and pours sugar into his coffee.

"Can we ever win?" he asks. "In a ring,
I know what to do. On the streets,
in people's homes, in Sussex County,
not so much."

NEW SCHOOL, NEW SCHOOL YEAR
THOMAS

I am an outsider at Weequahic High
My parents are not from eastern Europe
I pass through the hallways with heavy sigh

Without Benjy by my side, I don't try
To make new friends, only Nordland stands up
I am an outsider at Weequahic High

I could join clubs, for sports teams apply
I throw a javelin, master chin-ups
But pass through the hallways with heavy sigh

I sit on bleachers, watch games, hands on thigh
Talking smack with Nordlanders, all keyed up
I am an outsider at Weequahic High

This high school should mean I should gratify
My interests, boost college-bound send-up
But I'm an outsider at Weequahic High

And you, Benjy, stand there in my mind's eye,
Reminding me of our friendship blowup
I am an outsider at Weequahic High
I pass through the hallways with heavy sigh

MA WANTS ME TO JOIN THE DEBATE TEAM
BENJY

I want us all to get along
to make Newark a safe place.
To do that means we've got to fight
against hatred, because there's no room
for hate when our houses sit next to each other
and our mothers stand in line at the grocer's
or for the bus downtown.
I imagine Pop's boxing gloves
on my own hands, but honestly?
I think that verbal jabs—

    Kapow! We have just as much right to be here.
    Thwack! You wanna argue? I've had Talmudic
        training. I can talk you in circles.
    Zowie! I'll send for Jewish gangster Longie Zwillman—
could be far more powerful.

GROUNDED
THOMAS

Buried am I in a mountain of high school homework.
Buried am I in the crucible of Nordland commitments
        that last beyond summer.
Buried am I in the lies I want to tell Father and Mother
        and the lies I tell myself.
As each day passes, I become less and less of my
        Newark teen self
and more and more of a uniformed, German-speaking
        son of New Germany.
Buried I'll forever be in a mound of manure
        I won't be able to escape.

I'VE MADE THE TEAM OR SO I THINK
THOMAS

Mother sets out pie
for dessert. I don't take a slice.
Father notices. "Eat what your mother
has made for you."

"I'm in training, Father," I say.
"I made the track team!
I threw the javelin farther
than any other kid."

Without looking at me,
he says, "Of course, you did.
That's your Nordland training.
You will not be on this Jew School
team. You will save your strength
for Nordland."

Mother shakes her head. There's
no room for defense. I excuse
myself from the table and go
to my room. I don't bother
to turn on the light.

A MINUTEKID IS BORN

BENJY

October 1937

"Not for nothing," Mr. Arno says,
"but kids don't belong here."
I follow Pop into the club.
Mr. Arno says, "You're not old enough.
How old are you?"
"Fourteen," I say.
He walks right up to me,
so close he could catch my breath.
"Fourteen," he says. "Well, maybe you can be a Minutekid,
our mascot." He turns to Pop,
"Harry, your kid know any of those
at Camp Nordland?"
"Yeah, Nat. The Anspach boy, Tommy."
I say, "He calls himself 'Thomas' now, Pop."
Mr. Arno rolls his eyes. "We don't want
any kids hurt. They're just kids
doing what they're told."
My head says, put up your dukes,
keep your chin up. Let's get
Tommy out of there.

I GET MY BEST IDEAS IN THE SHOWER
BENJY

I let the water from the showerhead
drape me in a cooling soothing blanket.

I let ideas percolate as I suds up, how
to rescue Tommy from Nordland.

I can't do it alone, just like water alone
won't get me clean. Water alone

can only go so far. I need a washcloth,
soap, a towel. And lots of water pressure.

The Minutemen won't care about kids.
But kids will care about kids.

I finish up in the shower, towel myself
dry, and put on clean clothes.

I pull out my trusty composition book
to jot down my thoughts about the Minutekids.

I won't be the only mascot.
We'll be a team of mascots, a team of fighters.

THE MINUTEKIDS OF NEWARK ARE BORN
BENJY

"What do the kids at school say about Nordland?"
Mr. Arno asks. "The German class divides into
Jews and non-Jews," I say. "And your teacher?"
"He's one of us. And he's German. Came
to America in 'thirty-three." "A refugee," Pop says.
"I got an idea. You—" Mr. Arno points
at me. "Recruit Jewish kids who want
to knock some sense into your former friends."

"The Minutekids of Newark," I say. "Yeah,
I could do that. We could make posters,
hold meetings. We will fight
for our right to be heard.
We are the Jewish kids of Weequahic."

SOLIDARITY
BENJY

Word of mouth spreads around Weequahic High
and Mr. Zucker's classroom fills with kids,
freshmen to seniors. Mr. Z nods at me
and I stand next to him behind his desk.

"Hi, everyone. I'm Benjamin Puterman, son of Harry Puterman,
boxer and Newark Minuteman. I'm pulling together this group of
Minutekids to help restore democracy to Newark."

I exhale so hard I can almost feel a rib crack.

"Down with Nazis!" one kid in a green sweater yells.
"I'm with you, Benjy," another calls out from the back
        fist in the air.
"What's the plan?" a third asks simply.

And there he's got me.

THE MINUTEKIDS PREPARE FOR ACTION
BENJY

"He's speaking *tachlis*," Morty says
after my big speech about bringing down
Camp Nordland.

"The unvarnished truth, this is what Benjy says,"
Mr. Z explains for the benefit
of the Gentiles in the room.

"From his mouth to G-d's ear," Morty says.
"But man plans and G-d laughs," Doris says.

I step back up to Mr. Z's lectern.
"Not this time. He won't laugh.
We have right on our side."

"And might!" Hildy adds.

Tachlis means I have to inspire
us into action.
Bubkes means nothing may come
out of it.

Here's the plan: We're now
a junior league under the Minutemen.
We'll start with pamphlets and flyers
to stop Nordland.

We'll fight in German class.
We'll fight on the basketball court.
We'll fight in the wrestling ring.
We'll fight on the pages of the school newspaper.

Kids volunteer for one activity or another.
We're on our way.
I can't wait to tell Pop.

EASY TO CHEW, HARD TO SWALLOW
BENJY

"Are you *meshuganah*? Crazy?" Pop says at dinner.
"This isn't kid stuff, young pup."
"But it's the kids in our own school
who are going to Nordland, Pop!"
He cut into his meat. Chews
and chews. And chews.

A week later, out of nowhere, he says,
"I guess you're right."
After he takes a swig of apple juice, he says,
"What will you need from me
and the Minutemen?"

I'll have to think hard about that.

WHAT WE KNOW TO BE TRUE
BENJY

My grandfather's prayer shawl, a gift for my Bar Mitzvah,
knows it could still be true
that all humans value the same things:
Family
Traditions
Education

Pop's old boxing gloves, though,
know another truth:
Not everybody values the same things
and they try to knock each other out
with their own take on things.

MASKS
BENJY
November 1937

Thinking of you, thinking of me.
When I should be studying for my algebra test,

I see you in the hallways
thundering along like Thor

Ready to hand out pamphlets promoting Nordland,
the solidarity salutes you make with other Nordlanders.

Beneath your mask, I know Tommy's still there,
sliding into home base with ripped knees,

snorting soda out your nose when I make you
double over with my Popeye impressions.

That mask you wear now scares me,
a Mr. Hyde monster that swallows Dr. Jekyll.

I wear a mask now, too,
of courage to knock off your mask.

FOOTBALL RALLY WITH FATHER
THOMAS

Everyone's going to the big game on Thursday
against Hillside High.

> It's not even real football. What is the American word
> for the football the rest of the world plays?
> With the white and black ball?

Soccer, Father.

> What kind of word is that?
> It's *Fussball*, football.

We'll have a bonfire the night before.
Get all jazzed up to beat our rival team.
Rah-rah-rah! Let's hear it for Weequahic High.

> Must you cheer a Jewish school?
> Isn't Nordland celebrating Thanksgiving
> in some way? A harvest festival?
> You'll go to that instead.
> I'll drive you.

THANKSGIVING
BENJY

"The time has come," Pop announces,
placing his gravy-stained napkin on Ma's
heirloom tablecloth, the one with her grandmother's
cross-stitching. I roll my eyes and glance at Ma.
We know what time Pop means. "I'll start," he says.
"I'm grateful for having food on the table, a couple
of bucks in the bank, and a job. Mother?" Bubbe
looks up from her fruit compote. "Oy vey, why
must you do this? We were having such a nice meal.
Well, all right. I am glad I got a place to go
on Thanksgiving and that I don't got to make
the turkey. There, happy?" Pop nods. Ma's turn.
"I'm grateful we're all together and that our parents
had the foresight to leave Europe when they did."
"Here, here!" Pop says. Now it's up to me. "I'm grateful
for this meal and this family. I'm grateful Pop taught
me how to box. I'm grateful for movies and comic books
and Sol's." But all of this just makes me miss Tommy.
By next Thanksgiving, I'm going to be grateful I did all I could.

MOTHER SOOTHES AND SMOOTHS FOR OTHERS
THOMAS

The Bund's Women's Service keeps
Mother busy. She knits our socks,
irons tablecloths. She cooks
and serves meals at Nordland's restaurant.
She ties shoelaces for the younger kids
in her work to keep us all tied to each other.

But that means she's not home
when I come home from school.
She's not eating dinner with us.
She's not cooking for us.

I take an apple from the counter
and Father slaps my hand
so hard I can see his fingers
still in my skin.
"That's for the apple strudel
Mother is making for the Bund's
bake sale. You and I must
learn to live with less
for the good of everyone."
He pulls another beer
out of the icebox.

"It's just a stinking apple!" I say.
He smacks me again. "Watch
your tone with me, boy."

"Why don't you go have
another beer?" I say without thinking.
His punch knocks me to the floor.
It's just a stinking apple,
I mutter, as I crawl toward my room,
my stomach grumbling.

BRING IN THE HEAVYWEIGHTS
BENJY

If I could call on anyone to help the Minutekids,
I'd call on Errol Flynn. Quick-witted, fencing genius,
sarcastic, laugh in the face of death. We all need

that bravado to take our stand no matter the consequences.
If Errol's not available, we could use a tough guy like
Edward G. Robinson, a cigar in his mouth, a rod

in his hand, and no fear. If Edward G.'s not available,
we could use a charmer any person wants to trust.
Ma loves Clark Gable's voice and his dimples.

If Clark's not available, maybe Mr. Arno
could use his connections to get us
  Max Baer
  Maxie Rosenbloom
  Barney Ross

We Jews have a history of boxing.
Might as well put it to good use.
And I, as the leader, well, I'm a quick-witted
boxer who's fast on his feet, ready to anticipate
the opposition's moves.

MIGHT MAKES RIGHT
BENJY

Our fists hold our might
to make right and
fingers hold pens
to write words of might
words of right
through the rite
of making things right
in Newark. We engage
in the rite of busting
antisemitism, of separating
right from wrong,
of our right to speak,
to write with right hands
and left hands. We've got
might on our side to create
the right of way. It's our right
to clean up New Jersey.
Don't write us off.

SALTSHAKERS
BENJY

Light pours into the classroom through the gaps
of the shades. The dust fairies are having a field day,
flapping their tiny wings in a dance all their own.
This newspaper room is a mess. The floor is littered
with drafts of Minutekids flyers. Someone's knocked over
the wastepaper basket. A single chair leans against
the wall for support. I want to power my way
through this room, using my words in a right punch,
an uppercut, a left hook to the Nordlanders. That's
what I call them now, Tommy included, as if they're no longer
individual people. Even though this room is a pigsty,
we'll fight clean. Maybe. Then off to Sol's for sour pickles.

NO QUESTIONS FOR FATHER
THOMAS

I never ask Father why he came to America.
I never ask him why he stopped singing;
Mother said he could have been an opera star.
I never ask him why he chose Newark.
I never ask him about his brothers or sisters.
I don't even know if he has any, but Mother
says he does. I don't know if he went
to university, how old he was when he left home
or even where home actually was. I never ask,
I never mention Rudi's name either,
because I'm afraid I will upset him to the point
where he no longer knows my name. Mother keeps the radio dial
on the opera broadcast. We don't have a record player.
Wagner's operas always make Father feel stronger,
prouder, as Mother says, more like his old self,
when I could call him Daddy and he would
let me play horsey on his knee. When he called me Tommy.

LET'S GET READY TO RUMBLE
BENJY

Coming to you from Yankee Stadium,
it's pugilistic teen reporter
Benjy Puterman.

In this corner, heavyweight champion
American Jew
Max Baer
in red, white, and blue trunks

In the opposite corner, former
world heavyweight champion
from Germany, Hitler's own favorite,
Max Schmeling,
in red and black trunks

Fifteen rounds,
ladies and gentlemen,
the fight of the century
between two bears.
See what I did there?
Baer, bear?
I'm a regular Groucho Marx
or Eddie Cantor.

But back to the action.
Baer's making good
defensive moves.

Round ten, Baer deals
a terrific right, but

Schmeling won't give in.
Another right, and then another,
Schmeling topples. Down
for nine counts but stands up.
Schmeling's legs now rubber,
Baer gives him a right, a left,
jabs and uppercuts.
Schmeling holds on to the ropes.

It's all over, folks.

Baer wins!
Technical KO!
A win for the US of A
and for Jews everywhere!

DUELING FLYERS AND PAMPHLETS
BENJY AND THOMAS

We come into German class,
each armed with a stack
of mimeographed papers.

                    Why do we have a Jew teaching German?
                    Any of the adult members of the Bund
                    could teach us—and teach better.

Are Tommy's cheekbones more chiseled?
His mouth more determined?
His hair blonder and his eyes bluer?

                    I begin handing out my flyers
                    about our upcoming Christmas market,
                    a fundraiser for Camp Nordland.
                    I am selective.

"Come to our rally," I say,
passing out my material
to the Jews in the class,
which is mostly everybody.

                    We Nordlanders go through the aisles,
                    until we are chased. Papers fly everywhere.
                    Where is the discipline?

We cannot let them win.

WOLF PACK
BENJY

Tommy's running with the pack,
the taste of blood on his lips,

Hooking arms with Johanns, Gustavs, Rolfs,
follow the pack dog in front of you,

step here, that's right, don't go off
on your own. Stay with the program.

Tommy's running with the pack,
muscle memory moves on his hips,

Marching lockstep with his New Germany pals.
Bulge those limbs, be strong for the Führer!

Tommy's running with the pack,
the scent of prey in school hallways:

Who is strong and who is weak?
Who has might and who is meek?

Tommy's running with the pack,
melodies oompah in his ears.

Bring him back to Nordland's high grasses,
soldier camaraderie in the bunks.

Tommy's running with the pack
and I'm going to stop him.

Because once you run with the pack,
the hunt for blood never ends.

GLASSY-EYED FISH
BENJY

I once helped an old man cross
Springfield Ave. He muttered something
in Yiddish and patted my head, Grandma-like.
I thought he was going to pinch my cheeks, too.

The cheeks of the smoked whitefish
gleam in the light of the display case,
their eyes glassy. I wonder what
their last thoughts were
before the hook lifted them
out of the water.

You'd think the Passaic River,
dirty as it is, would protect us
from the Nazi Armada.
But they are here among us
with their false names and pledges
and Newark's Jews are just
dead whitefish in the display case.

SOUTHBURY SAYS NO
BENJY
December 15, 1937

The paper says the Bund bought
178 acres in Southbury, Connecticut,
for Camp General von Steuben,
named for the Prussian general
who trained Americans in the Revolutionary War.

The paper says this farming community
descended from Yankee patriots
put the kibosh, my words, on the whole thing.

Yesterday Southbury enacted zoning laws so Bund members
couldn't clear the land on Sundays.
There will be no Camp General von Steuben.

Why couldn't Andover have done this?

WHO AM I?
BENJY

In the bathroom mirror, I'm someone else—
a federal agent hired by the FBI
to scurry through Newark subway tunnels
and find the scum.

In the bathroom mirror, I'm gangster Longie Zwillman,
good to his mother and Weequahic Jews,
but let's face it, people, he's a mobster
no one wants to mess with, including the Bund.

In the bathroom mirror, I'm Sam Dickstein,
a big mouth with a big stick of Congress
to stop Fritz Kuhn and the Bund,
to stop the spread of Nazis in America.

In the bathroom mirror, I'm just me—
skinny, scrawny Benjy Puterman,
whose biceps look like Bubbe's
misshapen meatballs, whose flabby abs
wouldn't withstand a punch from
a roll of toilet paper. But the mind?
A regular Einstein, so my mother says.

THE CHRISTMAS MARKET
THOMAS

The Women's Service is at it again,
making all sorts of cookies and crafts
to be sold at the Christmas market,
festive warmth against cold winter's draft.

The Women's Service is at it again,
mothers and sisters bundled in coats.
They stand at their booths, eager to sell,
prepared on each customer to dote.

My favorite cookie is gingerbread,
I love the firm, thin bottom wafer.
If I'm lucky, Mother will keep some
home for Father and me to savor.

Nutcrackers, ornaments, hot mulled wine,
cloves and oranges, chocolates galore,
carved animals, felt hats, sturdy pipes,
Advent calendars with cardboard doors.

The Women's Service is at it again,
there's much to celebrate this season.
We're all in good health. Let's lift a glass
and toast—*Prost*! We've got a jolly reason.

SILENT NIGHT ON GOLDSMITH AVENUE
BENJY

I stand in the street outside
Tommy's home, wool cap
over my head and ears,
jacket zipped to my neck.

The Christmas tree stands
before the parlor window,
all lit up with white lights
and round ornaments.

Before Nordland, I'd be sitting
in that room, drinking hot chocolate.
Before Nordland, Tommy
would have a gift for me
and I'd have a gift for him—
A pen
A wallet
A key chain
A book
A record.

PART II:

PUSH AND PULL, 1938-1939

I'M A SEASONED CAMP NORDLANDER
THOMAS

The summer and fall were a blur of red, white, blue, and black. Most camps operate only in the summer, but then Camp Nordland is no ordinary camp. It's not just for kids. Parents rent cabins and enjoy the country life outside the city, the trees, the lake, and the beer. It reminds them of their homeland. Nordland is an American homeland. When I go to Nordland, often with Father, we are son and father, children of the German Fatherland on American soil. Germans love nature, Father has told me this many times.

Nordland is open all year round for special events. The next few months will bring President Washington's birthday; *Fasching*, the German carnival celebration before the restrictions of Lent; and the Führer's birthday celebration. Both Washington and the Führer are founding fathers of new nations, nations that will claim their new, bold futures. It's only a matter of time before the Führer realizes his dream of more land for the German people, the land we deserve. Every night Father drinks a toast to Adolf Hitler. The Führer's building roads and cars. He's finding people jobs. Mother says he's been a gift to the German people. She lifts a glass to his health.

WINTER DOLDRUMS
THOMAS
January 1938

I tramp through snow, and the pond
has frozen at Weequahic Park.
I long for the green fields of Nordland,
the flight of birds in tight formation
inspired by our ranks.

We'll still be brought to campgrounds
for Fasching in March, that celebration
of coming spring, and of course for the
Führer's birthday in April. We'll pay homage
with lines of respect in order of rank.

I can't wait for my second summer,
for my leadership skills to be noticed,
and to advance through the ranks.

SMOKED
BENJY

Smoke has settled in Tommy's eyes,
his gaze no longer clear. His school
binder notebook now carries an inked
swastika. He's not afraid to show
his allegiance. I noticed in assembly
he didn't place his hand on his heart
when we sang "The Star-Spangled Banner,"
especially, "land of the free."

I see Tommy on the bleachers
with a couple of his Nordland pals.
They're not even watching us
slaughter Irvington on the court.
Tommy's got a cigarette between his fingers.
Jeez, we're only fifteen. Does he think
it makes him look and feel older
or just entitled? The boys he's with,
seniors, have ciggies too and are blowing
smoke rings.

Me? I prefer my smoke
in lox or herring, preferably
with a shmear of cream cheese
on a fresh, hot bagel direct
from the bagel factory.

SMETANA'S *VLTAVA*
BENJY

I could sit here in assembly
and listen to this orchestra play.
I could remind myself the world
outside is a worse place than the auditorium
and Weequahic High.
I could close my eyes and recall
a snowball fight over the struggling cars
on Peshine Avenue.

I hear something in the music—
chords that remind me of hope.
Flutes sing of rippling streams.
They join and swell
into a melody that bursts my heart.
My mouth opens to catch
the river of two equals—interrupted
by tuba, timpani, and trumpet.

I snap out of my haze, back to my body.

I could sit here and do nothing.
I could step down from the Minutekids,
focus on my homework and preparing
      for college.
I could let Tommy go his own way.

DON'T MIX MILK WITH MEAT
BENJY
February 1938

Don't throw cream into my eyes, Bubbe says
when she knows I'm not telling the truth.

You think I don't know what you're up to,
Bubbe says, as she puts before me
a slice of pumpernickel bread
spread with shmaltz. The chicken fat
slides across my lips and tongue,
smooth and salty.

I'm not up to anything, I say,
and I almost ask for a glass of milk,
but that would make Bubbe shudder,
mixing milk with meat. That wouldn't be kosher.

I'm just trying to help a friend, I say.
She cuts two slices of her homemade
pound cake and puts them onto wax paper.
For your friend, she says.

If only I knew how to present
this gift to Tommy from my grandma,
the one whose pound cake he used to love.

You're a good boy, Bubbe says.
She pinches my cheek and puts a dollop
of cream on my cake—for later, she says.
Just don't mix the cream with the shmaltz.

EVERYWHERE
BENJY

Mrs. Hamilton tells us today
about the Trojan Horse that soldiers hid in
for a surprise attack on their enemies.

Only the horse is here—
riding our streets, pretending
to be ours but isn't.

How would I know if the guy at the butcher's
on Belmont or the woman eyeing a new hat
on Springfield isn't hiding their truth

in their own kind of Trojan horse?
How do I know they're not wearing swastikas
or "I Love Adolf" buttons underneath?

They could be on every bus,
in the movie theater watching Westerns,
riding the escalator in the department store.

Somedays I just want to run
to Bubbe's on Vassar
and dunk my face in the

big bowl of cut-up fruit
she keeps just for me. Strawberries
are my favorites. Somedays

I want to hide under her
massive oak bed. But then other days
I want to strut through

Weequahic High, swagger
like I'm stepping into the ring.
I'm a Puterman, son of Harry
"The Obliterator." It's what I do.

WHAT I OVERHEAR
BENJY AND THOMAS

I overhear Tommy talking about
Washington's birthday celebration
at Nordland. What do Hitler
and George have in common?
Nothing.

> I overhear Benjy talking about
> the family vacation the Putermans
> took for Lincoln's birthday
> because it fell on a Saturday.
> They drove to Washington, DC,
> to visit the White House
> and the Lincoln Memorial.

I overhear Tommy say the Anspachs
did nothing to celebrate Lincoln's
birthday. Well, why should they?
It's not on the Nordland plan, I guess.

> I overhear Benjy avoiding conversation about me.

I overhear Tommy snapping his books
shut instead of answering questions about me.

> I'm tired of listening.

THE FÜHRER AND GEORGE WASHINGTON
THOMAS

Do you think you've done as much,
President Washington, I ask silently,
staring at George's portrait at the front
of homeroom. Listen to me, George,
I'm talking to you. Do you think
you've done as much for America
as Adolf Hitler has done for the
New Germany?

This year's Washington's birthday celebration
will be held at Newark's Turnverein Hall,
Sunday, February 20. Leader Kuhn
is our main speaker. Our uniformed
service troops will serve as our protection,
our own police force.

George, you're pretty quiet. You may have
done a lot for this country over a hundred
years ago, but what have you done lately?

Let me tell you about Germany's leader.
I hope you're seated comfortably,
because this is going to take a while.

OH NO, THEY DON'T!
BENJY
February 18

Pop's in an uproar and so is Mr. Arno.
So are all the Jewish war veterans. "We've
got to stop the Bund's so-called celebration,"
Pop says. "It's so . . . so . . . un-American.
They're taking Washington as their own."
I know what they'll do. Bring their usual stink bombs,
brass knuckles, and pure grit to the hall
on Williams Street. "We tried it nice,"
Pop continued, "with letters of protest. At least
they've agreed not to bring in Kuhn. He
was supposed to be the key speaker."

"Can I go?" I ask. Pop looks at me
like I'm a double-headed carp.

CAUSE FOR CELEBRATION!
THOMAS
February 20

We march! I take my place with other
Nordlanders in our belted uniforms.

We march into the hall, led by
the fife and drum corps.

We march as 1938 and 1776 revolutionaries,
inspired by Adolf Hitler and George Washington.

We march past the speaker's platform
covered with swastikas and the American flag.

We march as the American flag
floating from the ceiling touches our shoulders.

We march past the portrait of Washington.
We march, ready for opposition!

We march to show
off our expert flag maneuvers!

We march, we celebrate!
We march, we sing "The Star-Bangled Banner"
with German accents.

ON THE WAY HOME FROM WASHINGTON'S BIRTHDAY CELEBRATION

THOMAS

Father lies:

Yes, the outfits you boys wear at Nordland are similar to those worn by Nazis,
but the Bund has no connection to Nazi Germany.

Yes, the uniforms and salutes reflect German-American custom.
We are not Nazis. We are National Socialists.

Yes, the Bund's principles might appear to resemble those of the Nazi Party,
but we absolutely and fervently support the American system of government.
I'm an American citizen now, after all.

Yes, "heil" is a typical German greeting
and has nothing to do with Nazi Germany.

WHO'S GOING TO WATCH OVER US?
BENJY
February 23, 1938

Left, right
Left, right
Nazism marches toward us.
Like ants to a picnic, they swarm
and chow down on our apple pie.

Pop says riots are going on
in Buffalo and Rochester, New York.
A bomb was thrown at a Bund meeting.

We need a group to watch over us,
to weed out the people who can harm us.
We need fences made of law to protect us.

Pop says Nazi leaders in America
have photos of our forts and bridges.

Pop says Dickstein's got photos
of the Nazi leaders.

Pop says Hitler made a speech before
the German parliament: he is ready
to defend the German people no matter
where they're located.

Left, right
Left, right
Nazism marches toward us
through open gates,
swastika boxers ready to charge the ring.

AUSTRIA JOINS GERMANY
THOMAS
March 12, 1938

"I am pleased to be able to tell you, gentlemen, that within the past
few days a further settlement has been reached with the country
with which we have a special affinity for various reasons. Not only
is it the same Volk [people]; it also has a long, kindred history and a
shared culture which link the Reich and German-Austria."
—Adolf Hitler before the German parliament,
February 20, 1938

Yet another victory for Hitler
and the Aryan race! Hitler's
homeland of Austria joins
with other German people
into a single nation, the
Empire to last a thousand years!

Troops marched onto Austrian soil.
Men, women, and children cheered,
saluted, and waved flags. One
big, happy people!

I WONDER
BENJY
March 12, 1938

"The Nazis regarded their goal of 'greater Germany' now an accomplished fact insofar as it affects Austria. . . . Austria has, within the last 12 hours, became an integral part of the German Reich."
—United Press, March 12, 1938

"Czechoslovakia today re-assured that any attempt by Germany to encroach upon her borders would be met with armed resistance."
—United Press, March 12, 1938

Hitler's troops announce they're coming home
to claim Austria for the thousand-year Reich.
I wonder what the Führer is having for dinner tonight.

Crowds cheer and salute to the stomp
of goose-stepping hobnailed boots.
I wonder what the Führer is having for dessert tonight.

But soldiers singled out Jews, cut beards and necks,
forced Jewish hands to clean sidewalks with toothbrushes.
The Führer is having Jewish deli morning, noon, and night.

CONVERSATION IN GERMAN CLASS
BENJY AND THOMAS

Must you do everything your father says?

Don't you?

But Pop will listen to me if I say no.

You'll just have to do it anyway.

(thinks)
Sometimes he'll change his mind.

Not my father.

No use in arguing.

FULL-BLOWN LIES
BENJY

Newark streets are full of hypocrites and bystanders.
"Isn't it terrible what's happening
to Germany's Jews?" they say, and then send their kids
to Camp Nordland.

IT'S PASSOVER
BENJY
April 15, 1938

It's Passover and we have an empty chair,
the traditional seat left for Prophet Elijah,
who visits all Jewish homes on this one
Seder night, recalling our release from bondage
and exodus from Egypt.

It's Passover and we have an empty chair,
where Tommy crumbled a board of matzoh
      into his soup,
where Tommy stuffed *charoses* of minced apples and nuts
      in his mouth to make chipmunk cheeks,
where Tommy fidgeted until it was time
      to find the *afikomen*, the hidden matzoh.
Now he just wants to hunt the Jews.

It's Passover and I take Tommy's seat,
and fold it up against the wall. We
will not go into bondage again. My
fists will prove it. Let Tommy go prepare
for Hitler's April birthday.

THE TASTE OF WATER
BENJY
April 15, 1938

I sit at the Seder table and Mom
passes me the hardboiled eggs. I take one
and await the bowl of salted water,
symbolizing the tears we shed during
our slavery in Egypt. I mash up the egg
so every spoonful carries some tears. Somehow
each passes the lump that's formed in my throat.

We are on spring break and Tommy
will be celebrating Easter and I guess
the resurrection of his savior. Will
any tears be shed? Does water mean rebirth?
Are we both swimming in known or unknown waters?
Last year, he sat at our table, now with
two empty chairs, one for Elijah the Prophet and one
for Tommy Anspach. And I sat
at his Easter table, unable though, to eat the ham.
Tommy hunted with me for the *afikomen*,
and I hunted with him for chocolate Easter eggs
hidden in the tall grasses of his backyard.

Now we hunt alone, left alone with salted tears.

CHAIN REACTION
THOMAS

It's Passover but I'm not sitting at the Puterman
table. I'm not spreading chopped apples and nuts on my matzoh.
I'm not eating matzoh balls. I'm not following along
in English in the book about the Jewish exodus
from slavery in Egypt. I'm not eating turkey
or roast chicken. I'm not hunting for the hidden matzoh.

No, it's just an ordinary night at the Anspach
house, just Father, Mother, and I. We are eating
schnitzel with noodles and an apple pie. "In just
a few days," Father says, "we will celebrate
the Führer's birthday
at Nordland." "I'll make scrambled
egg dumplings. I hear that's his favorite food,"
Mother says. Father approves by downing
three shots of schnapps in quick succession.

THE POWER OF PROTECTION
BENJY

Nailed to our doorjamb is an ancient mezuzah
to bless us and our house

like the painted blood of the sacrificial lamb
at Passover to protect against the Pharoah

and the plagues. But can the tiny Hebrew scroll
tucked into the mosaic oblong casing

grab a Nazi salute and render it useless?
Can it deliver a KO punch to wrestle

an angry, hateful fist to the ground?
Can it tell the difference between

a mask
and no mask at all?

HERR HITLER'S BIRTHDAY
BENJY
April 20, 1938

"Have you seen Tommy?" I ask
as I hurry from class to class.
Someone says, "He's in my homeroom.
He's absent today."

My face drops. My shoulders droop.
I forgot what today is.
Tommy's at Nordland.

Eating bratwurst
Stealing a beer
Saluting the Führer

I drag with me an invisible bag
of mental mines—practiced phrases
of what the Minutekids will preach today.

The words already appear on posters
we've posted by stairwells and lockers.

DEMOCRACY NOW!
THE ONLY RACE IS THE HUMAN RACE!

Somehow I'm going to let Tommy know
the Minutekids are going to win.

SHINE THE LIGHT
THOMAS
April 21, 1938

Yesterday to celebrate Adolf Hitler's birthday,
we gathered in the Bund hall to watch
Triumph of the Will—a documentary
of the Nazi Party rally in Nuremberg in 1934.

Der Führer boards a silver plane
from Berlin to the medieval city to the west.
Crowds cheer, young and old. Many boys
are dressed just like I am.

Like unexpected sunshine, der Führer
shines his light on the German people
gathered for this huge rally—
bigger even than the Bund rallies
in New York City I've heard about.

Like an unexpected rainbow after torrential rain,
der Führer brings hope to a weary people—
weary of defeat, weary of victimization.
Our colors grow stronger every day to span the heavens
and keep the sun's rays focused on us.

Father took the day off from work
to take me. At the end he said,
"Adolf Hitler is going to change Germany
and the world forever."

BUT AT HOME
THOMAS

After Father hoists a combination
of beer and schnapps
he snaps
at me. "You didn't pay
enough attention at Nordland.
This is our Führer we're honoring.
You need to show respect."

"But I did pay attention, Father,"
I insist. "When I say you didn't,
you didn't," he says. He staggers
to a stand, hovers over me. Sweat
coats his forehead and upper lip.
"You hear me?" He raises a hand.
I duck. His arm goes into salute.
This time.

SPRING BREAK
BENJY

Over spring break I think about
how Hitler breaks the Treaty of Versailles,
his tanks rumbling to the cheers of his fellow Austrians.

That old end-of-World-War-I treaty he thinks
broke Germany's back. So he aims to take back lands
that didn't even belong to Germany then.

Give me a break. There's nothing he won't do
to break his word to others. No foot on the brake
to expand Germany east and west and eventually over the Atlantic.

The Bund sets up these camps like stakes in the ground.
Hitler-loving crews break the earth with their shovels, clear
the woods for tents and buildings. Why couldn't Andover

say no to the Bund like Southbury, Connecticut, did? At breakneck
    speed Hitler
sets up for war. He's going to break through more laws and treaties
to get what he wants. Breakdown dead ahead, mark my words.

THE WEIGHT OF A WORD
BENJY

How much does one of Tommy's hate words weigh
and is it heavier than mine?
As an accelerated math student, can I formulate
an equation that will produce the weighted value?
I want to figure this out. Because
when Tommy says, "Jew," he spews it with
added spit to sink it to the ground,
crash through the floor into the dirt, rendering it
unable to stand. I don't know if I have any words
in my vocabulary, even as an accelerated English student,
that can lift "Jew" out of its earthy grave.

SUPERMAN!
BENJY
April 1938

It's not fair, I think, as I crunch on a sour pickle
from Sol's barrel. I don't have fair skin and fair hair
and don't go to Oktoberfest fairs and eat schnitzel
and pretzels and drink steins of beer. I wonder
if the fairs they hold at Camp Nordland reek
of stale tobacco stink like the counter,
seats, and walls of Sol's Luncheonette.

I open a new comic book from the rack,
Action Comics. The Superman!
By day, he's mild-mannered reporter Clark Kent.
By night, he's The Superman
with a blue costume
and superhuman powers,
fighting for fairness
in Metropolis.

If only the salty brine of pickle juice
could shift the scale of what's fair and grant me powers.
"Get any of that pickle on that book and you buy it,"
Sol says. Some fair-weather friend he is.

Superhuman—isn't that what Herr Hitler
thinks Germans are? All's fair in war
and you never know,
Superman could be Jewish.

LOOK OVER YOUR SHOULDER
BENJY AND THOMAS

If I look over my shoulder,
I see Tommy at his locker.

> If I look over my shoulder,
> I see Benjy hurrying to class.

If I look straight ahead,
I see myself easing into my homeroom seat.

> If I look straight ahead,
> I see hours of drilling.

If I look into the future,
I see a brotherhood that beats Nazism.

> If I look into the future,
> I see a brotherhood of armed bodies and blank faces.

If I look into the future,
I see Superman saving us all.

WE NEED FLEET FEET
BENJY

I want to be bold in my hunger
to right the wrongs I see. But I'm not
like the teens in Germany risking their lives
against the Nazis. I'm not ready to be arrested.
I'm not ready to waste away in jail. I'm not ready
to be murdered. I just want Camp Nordland
to shut down. We need fleet feet
to silently, secretly pad through the high grass
and signal each other in a wily way. We
have no authority. I want to be bold in my hunger
to repair the world, as Bubbe would say,
tikkun olam. It's my obligation to do that. Do we
just support Pop and the Minutemen?
I want to be bold in my hunger
to keep things the same. The world
is changing too fast. Europe is a mess.
Can't we all just get along?

LOST

BENJY AND THOMAS

On the way to school today
I spot signs: LOST CAT.
Some little kid had drawn
a creature with long legs,
extra long tail, and pointed ears
below the words. The signs
on construction paper
tacked to the bark
of every other tree.

On Saturday mornings
I used to wake up early and draw
at the kitchen table. I drew magic carpets
and hippopotami and colored
them in with crayon.

Now on Saturday mornings
I get ready for German school.

Should I make a stick figure
of Tommy? Glue a photo
taken with Pop's Brownie camera
of us eating watermelon
bigger than our heads?

If I had the time to draw, what would
I draw now? The fields of Nordland?
Our marches? Our rallies?
Or would I draw Benjy and me
eating watermelon bigger than our heads?

It's too late
for watermelon.

AT THE GATES
THOMAS
May 1, 1938

Father drives me to Nordland and we pull
through the familiar gates. "Look.
Thomas, at how the camp has grown.
It's twice the size of last year!"

More ground, more buildings.
More kids, more parents,
more parties, more beer.

"All that money you didn't spend
at the movie theaters owned by Jews
helped to build this place,
build our future!" Father says.

He takes a swig from a flask
I've not seen before. I wish
I was old enough to drive.

MAY DAY AT NORDLAND
THOMAS

Girls in white with neatly combed hair in barrettes
carry red lanterns lit up from within, Japanese style.
They pass by the main building with the large NORDLAND
banner. Sentries stand on the hill keeping watch.

The girls march proudly and soon they will
approach the flagpoles that are now
tethered with white streamers. The girls
will dance around the poles while
we watch. The lanterns distinguish
themselves against the eastern sky
where the sun has already set.

Although camp has not opened yet
for the summer season, I cannot wait
to return, to get out of the house
and away from Father and his rants.
I want to be on solid ground and lose myself
in routine so I don't have to think or feel.

The girls dance and I wish I could too.
But here
boys and men stand at ease, observing
and thinking about their next obligation.

TAKING A STAND
BENJY

I stand by the Passaic River, the silt
      gliding on the brown current,
      debris littering the banks.
I dream of clear water, clear banks.
No Nazi symbols or salutes
and Tommy returned to Tommy.

How can the Minutekids make things right?
How can we break the trance, the dance
      of Nordland?
No shields, no swords.
We need to listen for the next things to happen
in the gaps of Teutonic breaths.
We need to stand our chance.

PROOF
BENJY

Here's my hypothesis:
The American government says it has
shocking information to show just how
far and wide the Nazi movement is
in our country.
Evidence: operation of 32 Nazi camps
Evidence: 480,000 people associated
with these camps.
Evidence: photographs that men
in these camps march and salute
the Nazi swastika.

I submit this is a bigger problem
than even Sam Dickstein knows.
I submit that even President Roosevelt
better watch out.

RUN FOR IT
BENJY
June 1938

"Let's run with it," Mr. Zucker, our German teacher, says
in response to my idea to make up
flyers for the Minutekids. No runaround,
we mean business. Sure, the Nordlanders
are giving us a run for our democracy.
If the flyers don't work, I'll run another idea up
the American flagpole. While Tommy
runs through the fields of Nordland,
while his fellow campers run through
the pages of *Mein Kampf* and commit
the words to memory, I'm running up a tab
at Sol's rundown luncheonette, racking my brain
to run amuck with new ideas. I noticed Mrs. Hamilton
had a run in her stockings. A run, a path of connected
threads. That's what we need, a strategy of connected
thoughts.

We're going to have a run-in. This is no run-of-the-mill
threat. It's a promise. Nordlanders, you'd best
run away and hide before the Minutekids
run you out.

MORE!

THOMAS

More strength
More primal
More flags
        Red

More eagles
More swastikas
More lightning bolts
        Black

More space
More wingspan
More of us
        White

We are the Nazis of New Jersey!

HONOR
BENJY AND THOMAS

Honor my parents
Honor my heritage
Honor roll at school

Honor the Fatherland
Honor my German blood
Honor roll at school

Kiss the Torah
Earn Bubbe's cheek pinch

Raise my arm in salute
Earn ribbons in field competitions

Dream of my place
among Newark's Jews

Dream of my place
among Germany's faithful.

A PORTRAIT OF MY MOTHER, ELSE ANSPACH
THOMAS

Her belly once swelled with my balled-up
body. Her arms clung to the bedposts
as sweat dripped onto the linens and through
her dark, thick strands of hair splashed like
inkblots on the pillows.

One arm now raises in salute
and she wishes she could have done more,
borne more babies for the Reich. Her arm
stretches higher for each day of guilt
that only one child lives, while
the other arm mixes, bakes, and frosts,
marinates, roasts, and slices. Take
the fork and eat well, she says,
it's the best we can do.

A PORTRAIT OF MY FATHER, GERHARD ANSPACH
THOMAS

His long fingers are red and bony,
calloused by long hours of wrestling with wrenches
in bathroom and kitchen plumbing.
His knuckles, he says,
are always bent with arthritis.

I imagine him in his younger days
when his tenor dreams hovered
in tucked-away nightclubs. Maybe
he remembers those smoky moments
while swimming in the lake at Nordland.
Maybe with each stroke he remembers
a chord he once loved to sing. Maybe
he remembers he was happy once.
When Rudi was alive. When beer
and schnapps weren't his medicine of choice.

OUTRAGEOUS!
THOMAS
July 1938

"Outrageous!" Father yells from the parlor.
He's holding a letter from Camp Nordland.
He waves it in front of Mother.

"Beer prices! They're raising the price of beer!
They can't do that!" Mother tries to settle
Father down, hands him a shot of schnapps,

turns on the radio to the opera broadcast.
"And the cabin rentals! They're more expensive
now too!" He downs the shot like it's water.

Mother says, "It's all to help Nordland become
what it can be. Why shouldn't they want
to raise money to have a shooting gallery? Wouldn't

you like that, Thomas?" I really don't care.
I just want Father to stop drinking.

A FINAL ROUND?
BENJY

Mr. Arno has become a regular
at our kitchen table, always
with his fists balled up,
ready to pound the table
or the Bund. "You know
what's happening now, don't you,
Harry? Andover's playing
a new game. Sticking the Bund
and Nordland with a ton of
rules and regulations.

"Is that good?" I ask.

"It won't be long now, son,"
he says. "Andover knows
what's going on at this camp.
It won't be long now before
we can close down this place."

THERE'S STILL TIME
BENJY

If the camp closes now, Tommy and I
can pick up where we left off. We can
let watermelon juice drip down
our shirts, spit the seeds into the street.
We can toss a ball back and forth
and pretend we're real athletes.
We can cool ourselves off
at the movies and imagine
it's us fighting the pirates
with our swords.

HERE AND THERE
BENJY AND THOMAS

Lightning bugs stick to street lamps.

        Grasslands roll away from the road to the lake.

On our tree-lined street electricity
buzzes through overhead wires.

        A moonless night releases wild polka dots
                into a crowded sky.

Off in the distance, cars rumble
on cobblestone highways.

        Off in the distance, beer steins
           clang on the table.

Somebody's mother yells out her window, "Manny
Mandelbaum! The streetlights are on.
You'd better come home right now."

        Birdsong skits across the horizon.

In the dark, I pull the covers over my head,
flick on my flashlight and read
the latest *Amazing Stories.*

        In the dark we are alone
        but together, rubbing the ridges
          of a new era.

INDEPENDENCE DAY
BENJY
July 4, 1938

We sit on bleachers at Weequahic Park,
the sun setting behind the Orange Mountains.
Silence sets the tone for
blasting pastel pellets into the sky
like new constellations,
exploding freedom all over us
like a protective bubble,
that final boom of each blast,
the eruption of revolution gunpowder.

The fiery stars will do battle,
boxing it out in the Milky Way.
The Stars and Stripes will knock out
the German eagle, sending it back
over the Atlantic.

We sit on bleachers at Weequahic Park,
the sun has set behind the Orange Mountains.
We whisper, silence comes before the storm.

What is Tommy seeing tonight,
nestled in evergreen camouflage?
Will the fireworks send up a swastika?

ACROSS GOLDSMITH AVENUE
BENJY AND THOMAS

Nordland's closing

                                        No, it's not.
                    What would you know about it, anyway?
                    You're not allowed anywhere near there.

I got it from a reliable source.

                                        They're wrong.
                        Nordland is as strong as ever.

We're taking you and the whole camp down.

                                        You and what army?
                                        We've got our rights.
We can fight you Nazis.

                                        We can fight you Jews.

                        Be afraid.
                        Be very afraid.

SIEG HEIL!
THOMAS

With all the power and strength of the New Germany
Our shirts crisp and clean, our belts tight
We stand in our lines, one brother to the next
All hands raised to the Führer.

Our shirts crisp and clean, our belts tight
We learn the importance of discipline and obedience
As we unanimously raise our arms to the Führer
Row upon row of respectful teens.

We learn the importance of discipline and obedience
No one wants to learn the consequence of doing otherwise
We are cogs in the wheel, row upon row
Working together for the ideals of New Germany.

We are not here to take risks, we learn to obey
Strength comes from conformity and a higher power
That higher power is the Führer to whom we give our allegiance
And know for whom we will fight when it's our turn.

VALHALLA IS THE NEW WORLD ORDER
THOMAS

If we had horses at the camp, they'd be sleeping
in their stalls, gearing up for a new day.

    The bonfire flickers and flicks the ashes
    of Jewish-authored books into the sky.

If we had horses at the camp, they'd haul
our tools to the fields so we could work the land.

    The bonfire gives rise to Teutonic ghosts
    that fuel us with ancient bravado.

If we had horses at Nordland, they'd remind us
of their Teutonic ancestors who carried our ancestors
into battle and won against our mutual enemies.

    The bonfire aspires like sunflowers
    to the promise of the new world order.

WE LOOK
BENJY

"We're only here to get the lay
of the land," I say to the Minutekids.

The seniors park their jalopies
away from the camp so their
rattling mufflers don't give away
our existence. We creep up
to the fence, past the big sign,
NORDLAND. My heart pounds
as fast as a field mouse.

We're just here to look, I tell myself.
Won't Mr. Arno and Pop be proud
of our surveillance? After they get
over their anger at us disobeying them.
Because no one expects us.
No one expects kids.

One of us has a secret camera
built into a pair of
binoculars he borrowed
from his dad. He can't
tell us where his dad got it.

Campers strut in front
of a big building with instruments.
Girls sing in German.
Everyone salutes the Hitler salute.
They remind me of the Nazi soldiers

I've seen in newsreels. The uniforms.
The stomping in unison.

A chill courses through my body,
unlike any I've known before.
Because this is no newsreel at school assembly.
This is a youth army. In New Jersey.

ALONE IN THE RING
BENJY

It's a risk that we've come on our own.
It's a risk that we have no tools, no armaments
        except our fists and mouths.
It's a risk that we have no backup defenses.
It's a risk we're willing to take.
But in my mind's eye, I see Pop
        shaking his head,
        muttering, "Oh, young pup."

WE KNOW ENOUGH
BENJY

To crouch low by the fence
To immediately determine where guards stand
To lower our voices to beneath whispers
To keep our eyes wide open
        Our secret camera busy

IN A STRANGLEHOLD
BENJY

Someone
grabs me
by
the collar.
I'm
chok   ing!

can't
               breathe.

WE RUN
BENJY

I dig
my fingernails
into the hands
that bind me.

He lets go
and thrashes
me around
to face him,
a man in khaki,
wearing a leather holster
holding a gun.

"What are you kids doing here?
This is private property."
He speaks with a thick
German accent.

He pulls me away from the gate,
kicks me with his boots
to the ground, scraping
my knees and palms
on the gravel.

I want to fight back.
I want to remember all
that Pop has taught me.
Keep my fists up.
Keep my chin up.

But I'm just a kid.
He's twice my size.
He's carrying a gun.

"Get away from here,"
he says. "Never come back.
The police will arrest you."

The other kids scramble
around me. They help
me to my feet.

On the way back
to Newark,
we say nothing.

OUR HANDS ARE TIED
BENJY

How can the Minutekids muster control
and strike again against Camp Nordland
without facing the control of Andover police,
let alone the Bund, whom we really don't know?
We're just teenagers, more used to big bands
and swing than we are to a controlling billy club
or threat of arrest to bring us under control
and Lord help us if one of us loses bodily control
in the process. We're just teenagers.

Adults expect us to respect control and authority.
But what about when authority is wrong?
We're just teenagers from Weequahic High.

If I could sit at my desk and anti-Nazi leaflets
could just fly from that Weequahic desk,
through the hallways, dart along Newark's
downtown boulevards, on into Belleville
and Bloomfield, south to Hillside and Irvington.
If I could just exhale and let my words do their jobs
without leaving my seat, that would be great.

But I'm not sitting in a field of tulips
in Fantasy Land. I'm grounded in reality.
All we kids can do is throw words
on paper and through the air. We can't
throw physical punches or even
get near Nordland's grounds.

WHAT A FOOL
BENJY
August 1938

What kind of fool thinks
he can best the adults
with fists of dreams and dust?

What kind of fool believes
all it takes is chutzpah
to get past the world's longest hatred?

What kind of fool storms
Camp Nordland grounds
with no troops of his own?

What kind of fool? I'll tell you who.
Benjy Puterman, idiot extraordinaire.

BRUISED FRUIT
THOMAS

"Don't bruise the tomatoes!" Mother
yells as I carry her basket filled
with them from the car to
the Nordland cabin Father has rented.

As if I'm too clumsy or awkward
to handle them properly. Just
because I throw a javelin
with speed and accuracy
and just won a ribbon
at Youth Sports Day, it doesn't mean
I can't handle a thin-skinned blob
of seeds and pulp in my hands.

Mother hasn't noticed the bruises
on my arms and knees from the hard work
I'm doing at Nordland. Even if I have
thin skin, I can handle it all right.
I have to.

THE LIGHT OF TRUTH
BENJY

Newark streetlights turn on automatically
and all kids know they should come home.

But at Nordland, the leaders control
the lights, electrifying the chain-link fence

to keep others out
or to pen campers in.

I've seen enough gangster movies
to know the effect of light

on telling the truth.

If the camp leaders manipulate light,
they control the truth.

And without me to tell Tommy what's what,
can he make out the truth for himself

or just follow the path
of the moths to flame?

I TURN FIFTEEN
THOMAS
August 27, 1938

"Happy Birthday, Thomas," Father says.
I'm fifteen now.
Mother will give me school clothes, I bet.
Father will give me more of his advice
for free.

I'd like to believe he considered
A new bike
Magazine subscriptions
An allowance
A library card of my own

Maybe he already decided against
a trip to the Old Country
a hiking retreat to the mountains
a visit to Germantown, Pennsylvania.

What I really want
is to make my own decisions
to follow my own heart about what's right.
Is fifteen old enough to get that?

At dinner, after I blow out my candles
on top of the Black Forest cake
Mother baked and topped with cherries,
Father sings "Hoch sollst du leben,"
in that opera voice of his. His song
wishes me many years of life. Did he
sing that to Rudi? A lot of good the lyrics

did him. Mother hands me a box.
I open the tissue paper: a new blue suit.
Father hands me a box, too:
Not a bike
Not magazines
Not an allowance
Not a library card
but a new shirt and tie
and my own subscription to the Bund newspaper.

"Now you don't have to wait until
I'm done with it!" he says, so proud
of this gift that he's practically
drooling at the mouth.

I smile. I nod.
But later in my room,
I stick the paper under my winter
clothes stored under my bed.

HAIL TO THE FATHER OF OUR COUNTRY
THOMAS
September 4, 1938

Fritz Kuhn stands before thousands of us,
the end of our second summer at Nordland.
"We need to return to the strategies of George Washington."

I close my eyes and I am one with the pine trees.
My eyebrows lift toward the sky like eaglets
testing their strength.

Leader Kuhn pounds the podium on the word, "Germanic."
He says we are to build an Aryan government
      under the swastika.
"We need to return to the strategies of George Washington."

I close my eyes and my skin opens up
to let his words seep into its crevices.
They fill me up.

Kuhn says we have ideals we cherish.
We have goals for a racially pure society
      of white Gentiles
"We need to return to the strategies of George Washington."

I close my eyes and whispers of ash
knit together as armor at the back of my head.
All my fingers tingle with frenetic energy.

I am George Washington, surveyor of land.
I am George Washington, general of the patriot army.
I am George Washington, leader of a new nation!

Cheers for Leader Kuhn rumble
from ground to sky, my voice is among them.
And hail to George Washington!

A CONVERSATION ON THE FIRST DAY OF SCHOOL

BENJY AND THOMAS
September 6, 1938

"Can't you see what they're doing to you?"

                               "They're doing nothing. They're
                                       Germans like me."

"You're an American. Born right
here in Newark, just like me."

                                       "I'm not like you.
                                 We're different races."
                             (Scrutinizes Benjy's face)

"We are not different races.
We both belong to the human race."

                                           (cackles)
                     "There are tiers in the human race.
                                   I'm at the top.
                            You're at the bottom."

(my bones chill)
"How do you explain
Jesse Owens's Olympic win
in 'thirty-six, huh?

                                         "A fluke."

AN ENCOUNTER ON THE FIRST FRIDAY
OF SOPHOMORE YEAR
BENJY AND THOMAS

In the cafeteria line,
the lunch lady ladles
macaroni and cheese.

"Go on, do it!" the Nordlanders say.
I knock over Benjy's tray,
wet pasta and cheese sauce cover his shirt.

"What'd you do that for?"

The guys congratulate me with pats on the back.
They push Benjy away.
I push Benjy away.

I didn't even have a chance
to defend myself.

"He's just a Jew," one of the boys says.

He's not worth my trouble.

IT'S OVER
BENJY

I'm throwing in the towel,
watching it hit the canvas,
hearing the referee call the match over.

I'm throwing in the towel,
calling it quits. How many times
do I need to hit my head
against a brick wall and
expect our friendship
to be like it once was in grade school
or junior high?

I'm throwing in the towel,
giving up, admitting defeat.

So long, farewell,
auf Wiedersehen.

GOLD

BENJY
October 1, 1938

"Adolf Hitler's artillery, anti-tank and anti-aircraft rolled into
Czechoslovakia at dawn today, following infantry which had begun
the march for so-called liberation of the Sudetenland . . ."
                                    —Associated Press, October 1, 1938

If I could spin gold from straw,
I'd give some to Grandma.
I'd give some to Ma and Pop.
I'd ask Pop to deposit some
in my bank account to put
toward college. But all the money
in the world can't stop
the hobnailed boots of Nazis
marching all over the map,
from stealing gold teeth
from our German Jewish cousins,
and freezing their bank accounts.

Today the Nazis invaded
the Sudetenland. I looked it up
on a map. It's the area in the north
of Czechoslovakia where, Hitler says,
lots of Germans have been living
for hundreds of years.

The swastika
continues to spread across Europe.

MORE GERMANS IN A BIGGER EMPIRE
THOMAS

"Thousands of Sudeten Germans from Czechoslovakia crowded
into the square . . . to hail Hitler as their rescuer."
                              —Associated Press, October 1, 1938

Father and I are at Nordland
again, this time to celebrate
the annexation of the Sudetenland.
Somehow the facilities fit 4,000 of us.
Father beams as Leader Kuhn addresses us.
His cheeks puff up with pride like the
World War I medals on his old uniform.

Father says, "They've been Germans
all along. Now they can live again within German borders
without having to move from their houses."

I just take this as the Führer bringing
all Germans together as one people.
How can that be a bad thing?

WE STRETCH AND SPREAD
THOMAS

The span between the Reich eagle's wings is the same as a collection of our rolled-up fists. The span between the edges of the swastika is the same as the boundaries of the ever-growing Germany. The span between victory and defeat is faith in our leader, belief in our destiny, rights as Aryans as a higher-order people, and our boots, troops, and tanks.

LEADER KUHN UNDER ATTACK
THOMAS
October 4, 1938

I steal a glance
at my copy of the Bund newspaper,
telling Mother it's to practice
my German. For once she's home.

According to the paper,
Leader Kuhn left us at Nordland
to give a speech in Union City.
Protesters against the Bund
held signs that said DEPORT
FRITZ KUHN and FRITZ KUHN
FIGHTS THE BILL OF RIGHTS. They
threw bricks at him.

Americans are against us, me,
but I'm American, born right here
in Newark. If Leader Kuhn
is under attack, so is Camp Nordland
and so are we. Will I have to start
carrying a gun to protect myself?

How safe is anyone, anywhere?

THE MINUTEKIDS STILL STAND
BENJY

With Mr. Zucker's help, the Minutekids
prepare for an after-school rally. We make
posters:

> CLOSE CAMP NORDLAND
> NO NAZIS IN NEWARK OR NEW JERSEY
> SEND THE SWASTIKA BACK HOME

I write out a speech.

It's a Thursday and we stride
through the hallways decked
with our dictates. But a band
of blond-haired, blue-eyed
Nordlanders blocks our
entry to the football stadium.

I want to tell the Minutekids:
Fake them out!
We can get past them!

Instead, I bob and weave
in between them and the Minutekids
follow my moves.

Brains will always win
over pure brawn.

THE RALLY
BENJY

Up on the platform sit our invited
speakers from the veteran organizations:
       Jewish War Veterans
       American Legion
       Veterans of Foreign Wars

Each pledges a commitment
to close down Camp Nordland,
to kick Nazi sympathizers
across the Atlantic.

Hurray!

Mr. Arno is there, too,
speaking for the Anti-Nazi League.
He makes his purpose clear:
The Newark Minutemen,
sponsors of the Minutekids,
will do whatever it takes,
working with whoever it takes,
to make Newark and New Jersey
safe from Nazism. He can't help
but pound his fist into the podium.

Hurray!

It's not kids we're trying
to influence. We have little
power. We can't vote. It's

faculty and staff, community
members we're seeking. We
start a petition and pass it around
for signature.

I just hope we'll have enough
to force the camp to its knees
so we can finally shout

Hurray!

IN NEW MILFORD
BENJY

It's the main event, folks!
Benjy Puterman here, reporting.
The Newark Minutemen
enter New Milford to crush the Bund.

We're up against twenty police and firemen
armed with tear gas. No bell sounds
the round, there is no referee.
But the match begins when someone
throws a rock through the window
of a Bund leader's home.

The wife comes out and says,
"You Jews only know how to destroy!"
She flings a torrent of broken
glass at us. Illegal move!
No authority cares.

ROCK

THOMAS
October 10, 1938

Father and I are in New Milford
at a Bund meeting. I try to concentrate
on the speech, but all I hear is the commotion
outside, a mix of protesters and police,
firemen, too. My heart skips as a rock thrown
through a window shatters the glass
of George Washington's portrait,
like the one that hangs in every classroom.
Before we can even react, firemen turn hoses
on the protesters. I run to the window
and could swear I see Benjy and his dad.

THE MORNING AFTER
BENJY

Who am I to say
who chased the New Milford
Bund leader to the nearby pond?

Who am I to say
whether he slipped in
or someone threw him in?

Who am I to say
this is why the Bund leader's wife
left for Berlin?

SILENCE
BENJY

The sound of my loneliness keeps me awake.
It buzzes in my ears, whirls around my brain,
whispers without apology.

The sound of my loneliness chomps like
the pencil sharpeners in our classrooms.
A hunger that the school cafeteria's offerings

can't satisfy. The sound of my loneliness
is like a smoke-emitting bus on Broad Street
or the Weequahic High Marching Band

at the big football game against Hillside.
It's the sound of the tuba and the timpani
drum, the sound of noisemakers on Purim

when we drown out the name of the hated
tyrant Haman. The sound of my loneliness
is a song on the *Hit Parade,* the bass turned

way up that both Ma and Pop put their
hands over their ears and tell me
to turn down the radio.

How do I tell the sound of my loneliness
to shut up and go bother someone else?

GERMANY HAS GONE CRAZY
BENJY
November 11, 1938

"Nazis Smash, Loot and Burn Jewish Shops and Temples . . . Jews
Are Beaten, Furniture and Goods Flung From Homes and Shops"
—*New York Times*, November 11, 1938

Glass, broken glass, fills the sidewalks
and streets as non-Jews throughout
Germany and Austria look on,
even smiling. That's the way I see it
as I read Pop's paper.

Glass, broken glass, is the result
of vandals attacking Jewish stores,
synagogues, and houses.

Glass, broken glass, all because
some Jewish kid whose parents
were deported from Germany
back to Poland shot a Nazi diplomat
in Paris. He was just a kid, seventeen.

There's got to be more to it.
This had to be planned all along.
Nazis were just waiting
for an excuse.
I think of all the Jewish-owned
stores throughout Newark. What if Nordland campers
went through the streets with clubs and crowbars,
and smashed all the windows. Would Tommy be one of them?

I push my plate of scrambled eggs away.
"Pop," I say, "it could happen here, couldn't it?"
He says, "I don't even want to think about it.
But don't worry, young pup, we've got the Minutemen
and Mr. Dickstein, heck, even the FBI
is on our side!" Ma knocks on the wooden table
three times and spits at invisible demons,
At school, everyone,
especially those with family still over there,
is talking about the *pogrom*,
the Russian word for an attack
against the Jews.

And every time I hear a soda or milk bottle break,
I think our own night of broken glass
could start right here in Newark.

KIDS JUST LIKE ME
THOMAS
November 11, 1938

Hitler Youth boys ransacked
Jewish homes, synagogues, and shops.
They wore uniforms just like mine.

They used knives and clubs,
broke glass
destroyed furniture
set buildings on fire.

Crowds gathered to watch.
The fires must have been glorious.
First came the laws that stripped Jews
            of being true Germans
Then came laws that outlawed
            them working as doctors and lawyers
More laws that expelled Jews from German schools

Germany wants to rid itself of its Jews.
And here I am at Weequahic High
where I am in the minority. Mother
wants me to transfer to St. Benedict's,
but Father doesn't want to spend the money.
His drinking is more important.

IS DESTRUCTION THE ANSWER?
THOMAS

When I think of my future,
I see uniforms and conformity

When I think of my future,
I see no goofing off, only

laughing at victims' expense,
joy in other people's pain,

inflicting other people's pain.
I toss and turn at night,

seeing myself in shadowed alleys,
breaking windows, beating Jews.

This is not who I am,
not who I want to be

when I think of my future.

I'LL FIND A NEW BEST FRIEND
BENJY

I know lots of kids now
I didn't know before. Kids
like me who have seltzer
spritzer bottles in kitchens
and basements. Kids like me
whose parents switch
from English to Yiddish
when they don't want us
to understand. Kids like me
who worry about the Jews
of Germany and Austria.

I can find a new best friend,
a kid with whom I'll better blend,
a fellow Jew who'll comprehend
and fend off the hatred toward us
from the direction of Nordland.

"MA'OZ TZUR"-"ROCK OF AGES"
BENJY
December 17, 1938

I've been singing this song in Hebrew school
for years, but now the words in English
hit me in the gut like a sucker punch. The
song is about faith in fighting against
enemies and earning victory. See all
men free and tyrants disappearing. We
are tethered to our past, we are knotted
to our ancient traditions. Traditions that anchor
us and let us rise above the *mishigas*,
as Bubbe would say, the craziness.

I'm still thinking about rocks when Ma lights
the Hanukkah candles on the first night
of the holiday, celebrating the miracle
of a bit of oil lasting eight days as the Maccabees
fought against their enemies.

Rock of ages, our faith broke the sword
when our own strength failed us.

WHAT FALLS FROM ABOVE
THOMAS

The night is still and silent
as a heavy snow drops on trees and roofs.

I stare at the bedroom ceiling.
A spider drops down from the light fixture.

That's me.

I'm a spiderling caught in a web,
the silk strands woven by Camp Nordland

bind my wrists and ankles. They're
beautiful yet dangerous, and I could

lose myself in how
the strands reflect the sunrise,

how they blow in the wind but
never unravel,

how raindrops adhere to them—
or are those my tears?

IT'S NOT THE SAME
BENJY
Winter Break, 1938

Hymie Lieberman's been coming
to my house every day during
winter vacation. We play
Monopoly and cards, read
comic books and science fiction,
grab cherry Cokes at Sol's.

But the conversation goes like this:
What do you want to do?

       I dunno. What do you want to do?

I'll do whatever you like.

       What?

Huh?

And then it's time for Hymie
to go home for dinner
and we're both relieved.

ANOTHER PORTRAIT OF GERHARD ANSPACH
THOMAS

Father stands at attention in his Nordic
knit sweater with the metal brackets
fastened across his chest. All he needs
now is a familiar German opera on the radio,
his Meerschaum pipe, and his stein of
dark beer. Why did he even come to America?

If he and Mother had stayed in Germany,
I'd be a member of the Hitler Youth.
Father would be wearing a Nazi Party
button on his chest and Mother
would be doing exactly
what she's doing now. Serving the men.

I wonder if Father is trying to recapture
his youth, to roll back time before
Hitler, before Rudi, before the Depression,
when he'd go hiking in the mountains
with his backpack and his friends
to contemplate their bright futures
looking down into vast, bountiful valleys.

IT'S FOR FATHER I DO THIS
THOMAS

I am a puppet
pulled by Father's strings,
jumping at the chance,
the privilege to attend Nordland.

I am a puppet
without a will of my own,
bending to Father's whims,
because I want to see him smile.

I am a puppet
prancing on a stage for spectators,
tucking my real feelings
into the grain of my wood.

I TRY AGAIN FOR A NEW BEST FRIEND

BENJY

January 1939

This time I choose Lenny Sternberg.
His father's also a Minuteman.
We spar against newly built
snowmen, knocking off
their hats and carrot noses.

But then homework piles up,
and it's too cold outside to goof around.

THE THIRD TIME IS NOT THE CHARM
BENJY

I drown my sorrows
in an ice-cream soda at Sol's.

Another kid sits at the counter,
turning the pages of an *Action* comic.

This could be it!
This could be my new best friend!

"Hi," I say. "I'm Benjy Puterman.
You live around here?"

I can see it all now. We
hang out together,

swapping our stacks of comics,
doing the double feature

at the movie theater for a nickel.
He'll come to my house on

Friday nights to share our roast chicken
and I'll go to his house to share his meal.

The kid picks up his head, sips
his soda, "Nope, just visiting."

He jumps off his swivel chair
and joins a man with gray hair

at the cashier.
I'll just have to face it.

There's only one best friend
intended for me: Tommy.

ORDINARY PEOPLE
THOMAS
February 20, 1939

"A grand day!" Father says as we ride
the bus downtown to Penn Station. "A rally
at Madison Square Garden!"

"But I'll miss a day of school," I say.
No one's as reliable as Benjy for catching
me up when I've been absent. I found that out
last year for the Führer's birthday.

"No matter. Hearing Leader Kuhn
in person is more important," Father says.

In Penn Station a businessman rushes
with his attaché through the exit doors to Broad Street.
A woman with a hat bigger than our radio console
sashays in front of us, her rose perfume lingering
a bit too long. I don't see any other Bund members.
Father wears his Bund uniform,
but we're not at Nordland or a Bund meeting,
and he looks like a soldier,
a war-mongering soldier.
I thought we were ordinary people,
but maybe we're not.

"This will be a grand day," Father says as we ride
the train to New York. "A day to remember."

AT MADISON SQUARE GARDEN
THOMAS

Uniformed troops stand at attention
beneath the bigger-than-life, full-length
portrait of George Washington. We celebrate his birthday.
The Garden is packed to the 20,000-seat limit.

The troops continue to stand at attention
while the fife and drum corps play.

A Bund speaker introduces Leader Kuhn:
"We love him for the enemies he has made."
Enemies?
What enemies has he made?
Why should we love him for that?
I've already lost Benjy. I've already lost any Jewish
friend I had before Nordland.

Leader Kuhn begins his speech. Surely
I've heard him before, but now I think
I'm hearing him for the first time.
Down with the Jews!
Down with the Communists!
They are the cause of America's problems!
They control the press!

Banners wave:
"Smash Jewish Communism"
and "Stop Jewish Domination of Christian America."
I know Nazism beats against the Jews,
rails against Communism. I've read it

in *Mein Kampf*. But now surrounded
by it in words as big as my body
in English, it takes on new dimension
like a tidal wave that will wash over me.

UNTIL NOW
THOMAS

Until now, I've been tied to Father,
tethered to his ideas and his commands.

How do I loosen the knots that bind me?
How do I release myself?

Kuhn up there on the platform,
with all the pomp and pageantry,
the banners rippling like whitecaps
in a sea opening before me,
wild waves dancing, ever higher and stronger.

There is no path through the water.
Father's eyes gleam with Kuhn's every word.
Father steps into the waters and dives.

Do I follow him because he's my father?
Do I follow him because he expects me to?
Do I throw a life preserver after him and pull him back?

My head swirls even though I'm seated.
What am I doing here, in this place, with these people?

OVERCOME
THOMAS

I want to run out of the Garden,
but it's too big, too overwhelming.
I don't know my way around.
Father grabs hold of my arm.
"Thomas," he says, "are you all right?"
As if he actually cares about me.
I'm just a shadow. All I'll ever be
is a shadow of the son he really loved.
"Maybe you need some air," he says,
lifting me out of my seat. In his tow,
I stumble to the exit of our section.

We're alone now.
Alone.
Alone on concrete.
Alone where our voices will echo.
Kuhn's voice penetrates the walls.
The walls are closing in on me.
"Vati!" I scream.

UNCONSCIOUS
THOMAS

I am lying alone on the sand,
naked, curled up like a baby.
Waves creep toward me again
and again until the moon
pulls the tide away.
I am cold. The world
is silent except
for the rush of water,
a cleansing water
a rebirthing water
a baptizing water
"Welcome back
to the world,
Tommy,"
the waves whisper.

A CLOSE MOMENT
THOMAS

I come to and I'm a wet mess.
Someone has poured water on me.
A crowd has gathered around me.
There is Father, brow furrowed.
"Son, are you all right? You blacked out."
He helps me up,
brushes the soot off my pants.

Did I hear him right?
Did he call me "son"?

THE MOMENT WITH VATI VANISHES AND FATHER RETURNS

THOMAS

"I don't want to come to these
rallies anymore," I say
on the train home.

"I don't want to attend
any more Bund meetings,"
I say on the bus to Weequahic
from Penn Station.

"I don't want to go
to Nordland anymore,"
I say when we enter
our house.

Father glares at me.
He raises his hand
and I think he's going
to smack me,
smack me so hard,
he'll knock me out.
But all he does
is reach for a beer.
Barely audible, he says,
"As long as you live
under my roof, you live
by my rules. You do
as I say. Go to bed."

Like a deflated balloon,
I do. I never want
to go to the Garden again.
Never want to take a train again.
Never want to tell Father
how I feel
again.

FAULTLINES
THOMAS

We are all flawed, Mother says,
and I believe that's true.
Mother's flaw is her kindness
that she feels for everyone.
Father's flaw is his narrow-mindedness,
His belief in just one way:
>One way to think
>One way to behave
>One way to be loyal

My flaw is knowing that my parents
are flawed and their flaws
created me.

ANOTHER INVESTIGATION CALL
BENJY

Mr. Arno is once again sitting
at our kitchen table, this time
cracking walnuts with his bare hands.

"Sam Dickstein made another call
in Congress for investigation of the Bund,
because of the Madison Square Garden rally,"
he says. "I like Sam Dickstein," I say.
"Me too," Mr. Arno says,
handing me a walnut.

DO WE SAY THE MOURNER'S PRAYER FOR NAZIS?

BENJY
March 1939

"Hoo-hah," Pop says. "Kuhn is out
of the picture. He's been arrested
for tax evasion. He's off to the Tombs,
a prison in Manhattan."

"Will Camp Nordland close down now?"
I ask. "It won't be long now," Pop says.
But I've heard that before. Not that
I should care. I've given up on best friends
in general and on Tommy in particular.

THE WORLD'S A SERIES OF PUNCHING BAGS
BENJY
March 15, 1939

"The armies of Germany and Hungary early today swarmed across
Czechoslovakia, seizing cities and towns to take full control of the
nation."   —United Press, March 15, 1939

"Germany failed to notify . . . Britain, Italy, and France before taking
over Czech territory."   —Associated Press, March 15, 1939

In the gym of the world
stands a boxing ring.
Above the ring hangs
a series of punching bags,
representing the countries
Adolf Hitler has taken over
> Austria
> Czechoslovakia
More bags to represent
countries he's friends with
> Hungary
> Italy
> Japan
And yet more bags
of those who oppose him
> France
> England
> America
Where does the Soviet Union stand?
Where does Poland stand?

A contender enters the ring
from his respective corner.
Only one contender.
Adolf Hitler.
He takes Austria and Czechoslovakia
hits one, two.
He punches with all his might,
        his gloves protecting him.
The referees in swastika uniforms
            only blow their whistles
            when there's no air
            left in those bags.
Hitler leaves the ring, triumphant.
But you know he'll be back
        for more.

FATHER, IT'S ALL WRONG
THOMAS

Father, Leader Kuhn is in jail.
The Bund is done for.
Americans don't want swastikas here.
Can't you see that?

Father, Adolf Hitler is a madman.
Surely, you've heard that,
read that in the newspapers.
Can't you see that?

Father, it's all wrong.
I should not go to Nordland.
You should not be a Bund member.
Can't you see that?

But instead of listening to me,
Father falls asleep with
a beer in his hand and his
head in his Bund newspaper.

CROOK OR KUHN
BENJY
April 1939

"New York may do the job for us,"
Pop says. "Mayor LaGuardia wants
to kick Fritz Kuhn out of America,
cancel his citizenship."

Fritz Kuhn is a crook.
He was arrested for stealing coats
at the University of Munich in 1921.
Arrested, convicted, sentenced
to four months in prison.

Then he immigrated to Mexico,
worked in Detroit,
became a US citizen.

Sang "America" like the rest of us.

THE FBI STEPS IN
BENJY
April 7, 1939

After dinner, Pop pulls out
the evening edition of the paper:
"The FBI," he says, "has issued a report,
right here on page one. Says Irvington
is a hotbed of Nazi activities."

"With the FBI involved, this is
really good news," I say.

"Right-o, young pup. The report
says Camp Nordland is the largest
Bund camp in the country,
a center for Nazi propaganda.
The attorney general of the United States
says he's reopening the investigation
of the camp."

We clink our water glasses:
Here's to the FBI!
Here's to the attorney general!

I find out later the report
is already two years old.

THE MINUTEMEN TRY TO BREAK UP A BUND MEETING IN IRVINGTON

BENJY

Outside the Bund meeting
gather crowds of people and policemen.
Mr. Arno leads the Minutemen to the gate.

To protect the Bund meeting
the police form a chain the length of the fence.
"We don't want no trouble here," one says.

Mr. Arno insists, "It's un-American
what they're doing." He and the other
Minutemen push up, shove up

against the police. I do too.
We clinch and hold, no referee
is going to tell us not to. We're

here to claim the title
of knocking out the Bund
for good. But one police officer

sneaks a rabbit punch with his billy club
behind a Minuteman's head. He plays
drums on the Minuteman's belly. There's

no bell to sound the end of the round,
no referee to say stop the pummeling,
no trainer to pull him back into his corner.

There's only me—
"Pop!" I scream. "Pop!"

THE NEXT CONTENDER
BENJY

I don't see it coming—
the one-two punches from
the police.
> The sharp pain in my ribs
> My struggling to breathe

I don't see it coming—
me dropping to the ground
in a heap.
> I want my father
> I want my mother

I don't see it coming—
blood spurting from my mouth onto the pavement.
> Am I dying?

I
don't
see
anything

AT THE HOSPITAL
BENJY

Ma hands me a mirror.
I'm pretty beat up.

I'm bandaged like Frankenstein.
Bruised ribs. Black eye.
Black hole where a tooth used to be.

"No more Bund meetings," Ma says.
"What am I going to do with you and your dad?"
I try to smile but it hurts too much.

"You'll be all right, kid," Mr. Arno says.
"Your dad will be, too."

WHY DO I HAVE TO GO, FATHER?
THOMAS
June 1939

I want a summer of ball in the park
of ice cream and watermelon
and open fire hydrants in the street.

I want a summer of Superman
and cherry Cokes. I want a summer
of gazing through the gaps
in the oak trees at the blue sky.

I want a summer of
Playing, not drilling
Running, not marching
Swimming, not saluting.

"I don't want to go back
to Camp Nordland, Father,"
I say. "Heinz, Arnold, and Luther
aren't returning. Why should I?"

Father puts down his newspaper.
He glares at me as if curse words
came out of my mouth.

"Because I say so. Don't embarrass
me, boy." He picks up his newspaper.
Conversation's over. If indeed that was a conversation.

I WANT TO . . .
THOMAS

Cut Father down to my own size
Slice his words
Clip his high-and-mighty tone
Snip his demands
Tear open his facade
to reveal the father I once knew.

The Vati who held me on his knee
The pop who held my hand to cross the street
The daddy who came into my room when nightmares lurked

How did his skin grow
thick layers of arrogance?
How did he build up resistance,
fortify his immune system
to reject his own son?

CAMP NORDLAND'S LIQUOR LICENSE
THOMAS
June 30, 1939

"Where will I get genuine German beer now?"
Father asks.

Camp Nordland
is about to lose
its liquor license.
The Bund
is in a furor.
It's Andover Township's
decision now.

I like to imagine
Father in our parlor
listening to opera
without a beer in his hand.

I like to imagine he is smiling—
at Mother
at me
at his American life.

THE JIG IS UP
THOMAS
July 1939

"Cover up!" the group leader says,
handing us tarps to hide
the swastikas and eagles of the Reich.

"Hoist up!" the group leader says,
flying the American flag on the pole,
taking down the colors of the Reich.

"Strike up!" the group leader says,
as campers hug their drums, bugles,
and trumpets. "No German songs!"

"Man up!" the group leader says,
when a fellow next to me trembles
at the thought of a raid on Nordland.

"Give up!" I say to myself.
I don't want to be a part of this.
I want to go back to being me.

No matter what Father says.

THE MOONLIGHT TELLS NO LIES
THOMAS

Not that we have scarecrows in Newark
but I've passed them on the way to Nordland.
Bodies stuffed with straw and painted faces
where no real faces exist. Maybe a jacket
or coat hoisted up to monstrous heights
like Frankenstein.

I am a scarecrow with a painted face.
I stand in a Nordland field under
a half-moon, waiting for someone
to see the real me, to want to see
the real me in the moonlight.

But no one does and my head
hangs low when no one's watching.
In my head I hear Benjy's voice
making wisecracks about
the scarecrow in the *Wizard of Oz*
who needed a brain. If I had
a brain, I'd stand up to Father—
and even Mother—and tell them
to let me down from this scarecrow hook
of their expectations.

BRUSHSTROKES ON THE NEW JERSEY CANVAS
BENJY

Black, the smear of hatred
White, the leaflets we distribute
Red, our passion for the cause
Yellow, people who refuse to stand up against Nazism
Blue, New Jersey's finest policemen
Green, the peace that maybe one day we'll reach.

PUNISHMENTS

THOMAS
July 5, 1939

"Say one word in English,
and pay a two-cent fine,"
the section leader says.

"Disobey my order
and you'll get twenty lashes,"
the section leader says.

"Deface the pages of the Führer's *Mein Kampf*,"
and you'll go without food for three days."
the section leader says.

"Disrespect authority
and you'll   disappear,"
my bunkmates say.

THERE'S A BUZZ
THOMAS

Gossip and rumors travel like a swarm
of bees from bunk to bunk.

"We're done for!"
"The law is after us!"

Fewer boys and their parents
want to risk going against the law.

READY TO POUNCE
THOMAS

Goose-stepping days
grow stronger in Europe,
but here the lion of justice creeps from its pride
among Nordland's tall grasses.

Nazi uniforms fill the streets
of Germany, Austria, and Czechoslovakia
but here Jersey's new law forbids the uniforms.
The camp is weakening. Attendance
this summer has dropped. The law says

the camp can no longer show
the swastika, salute the Führer, or show
Hitler's face. Everyone knows

what goes on here at Nordland.
Congress knows, thanks to Rep. Dickstein.
The FBI knows.
The Sussex County Sheriff's Office knows.

The lion of justice is watching,
readying its mighty paws
to strike at the Bund's throat.

I'm getting out of here
before that lion pounces.

I DON'T WANT TO ANYMORE

THOMAS

I don't want to feel camaraderie in the brotherhood of khaki
I don't want to link arms and dreams with my bunkmates
I don't want to share in their sneers against those they believe are
subhuman
I don't want to join in good cheer when we win a tournament
I don't want to link their stories to mine by the fire
I don't want to share their insistence on being right all the time
I want to roam the streets of Newark
and be a city kid again.

DENIAL

THOMAS
July 14, 1939

Denied!
That Camp Nordland violated New Jersey's
anti-uniform law

Denied!
That Camp Nordland did not fly swastikas
or saluted in Nazi style

Denied!
That Camp Nordland spread racial hatred
materials

So, denied!
Nordland's liquor license.

RUNT OF THE LITTER
THOMAS

The morning, summer hazy,
gives me an early start with a run around the lake.

"What's that sound?" I ask myself.
I near lake's edge on the far side.
Rustling in the weeds. Then a whoosh.

Some camp leaders devised a pulley,
hoisting a puny boy in his underwear
out of the murky water.

Maybe he wasn't strong enough,
obedient enough. Maybe he was a burden.
He's not a burden anymore.

I CAN'T GET THE DROWNED BOY OUT OF MY MIND

THOMAS

Even if I close my eyes,
I can still see his sagging, bloated body,
that boy who paid a price.

Any one of us who questioned
Any one of us who failed to obey
Any one of us who dared to defy

Could be the boy in the lake.
I try to chase away the vision,
but the image remains stuck in my brain.

What if I didn't wear the uniform?
What if I didn't salute?
What if I didn't swear allegiance to the Führer?

Oh, Father, that boy in the lake
could one day be me. What would you do?
Do I need to sacrifice myself for you,
to make you see what Nordland really is?

SLIP, SLIP, SLIP AWAY
THOMAS

Have to get out!
Have to get out!

I wait until my bunkmates
are asleep, roll my uniforms,

illegal anyway, into a ball
and stash them under my bed.

Have to escape!
Have to escape!

I slip into normal summer clothes
and out of my bunk on this moonless night.

I make my way to the fence,
crawl under it, and stumble

out to the road. I stick out
my thumb to hitch a ride

as I pad toward the highway.
I can't see it in this darkness,

but I know it's there.
hanging on each tree I pass

I see the face of the drowned kid,
his skin falling off his frame.

I don't want to be the next victim.
Please, I pray, let a car come!

Rescue me!

CHICKEN
THOMAS

I don't know how long I've been
on this gravel road,

but I spy a two-lane road
now and a traffic light.

Now someone will surely notice
my outstretched thumb.

If Father knew what I was doing,
his face would redden like cabbage.

A truck rumbles along the road.
The window rolls down.

"Where you heading, son?"
        I nearly laugh.

A stranger calls me son
faster than my own father.

"Weequahic."
"Hop in. I'll take you

as far as the poultry market
on Prince Street."

YELLOW NO MORE
THOMAS

The truck is full of live chickens
and that foul raw chicken smell.
They squawk, their beady yellow eyes
and yellow beaks poking at me,
asking why I'm a refugee,
what am I escaping?
I meet their eyes and whisper:
Camp Nordland won't break me.
Camp Nordland won't grill me.
Camp Nordland won't twist me anymore.

ON MY WAY
THOMAS

I figure I can find a bus
from Broad Street home.
No, not my home.
The streetlights are on when I
stagger off the bus. Good,
the lights are on at the house. I bang
on the door.
It opens.
"Benjy, I have to tell you."

AT BENJY'S
THOMAS

I tell him everything.
I tell him what a day at Nordland
is like. I tell him about the rigor
and discipline, the drilling.
I tell him about the kid
in the lake. I begin to bawl
like I am five years old.
He says nothing.
Then I say,
"I'm so sorry. I know I've let
you down. We haven't talked,
really talked. Father said we
couldn't be friends."
He says nothing.
"I've been so stupid. Why
didn't you tell me that?" I say.

I expect him to grin his goofy smile.
I expect him to show me his latest
          comic book.
But he says nothing. Does nothing.
Except close the door in my face.

HOW STUPID
THOMAS

Why did I naively think
we could just pick up
where we left off
before Camp Nordland?

Why did I expect Benjy
to just forgive
all the mean things
I said and did?

How will I ever make amends?
Nordland is ripping me apart!

CLOSED DOORS LEAD TO CLOSED MINDS
THOMAS

The door is locked and I ring the bell.

    Mother comes to the door
    and puts a hand to her face.
    "What's wrong? Why aren't you at camp?"

I kiss her hello and spot Father
in the parlor reading his Bund newspaper.

"We need to talk," I say.

    "I'll get you something to eat," Mother says.
    "Some leftover roast pork and potatoes."
    She hurries into the kitchen.

A silence hangs like a shroud
between Father and me.
"We need to talk," I repeat.

                "Why are you here?" he asks,
                "and where is your uniform?"

"Father, do you know
what goes on at Camp Nordland?"

                 "Have you been drinking?" he asks.

"No, you do enough of that for both of us."

He smacks me so hard
I fall to the ground.

"Go ahead," I scream,
my face as hot as a winter fire.
"Beat the living daylights
out of me. It won't bring
Rudi back. It won't bring
your honor back. It won't
make a Nazi out of me."

SMACKDOWN
THOMAS

"You must go back!" Father insists.
"I will drive you back right now. Where is your uniform?"

Smack.

"Don't you know, Father? Don't
you know the law? It's illegal
to wear the camp uniform.

Smack.

"Don't you know, Father?
It's illegal to salute the Reich.

Smack.

"Father, if you haven't noticed,
you're in America, for god's sake!"

I'm lying on the ground now.
I'm down, but don't count me out.

It's time for me to face
the enemy:
No more uniforms
No more crewcuts
No more blind faith.

THE NEXT NIGHT
BENJY

I can't fall asleep without seeing
Tommy's face, his surprised look,
the hurt in his eyes, his falling apart

in front of me. He came to me for help.
I did nothing. I was so stupid. So full
of my own principles and my own hurt.

I slip out of my pajamas
into street clothes
and steal out the front door.

I ring the Anspach doorbell.
It's only about 10:00 at night.
Mr. Anspach turns on the porch

light. He peers through the window.
He opens the door a crack.
"I'm looking for Tommy,

Thomas," I say. "Is he awake?"
Mr. Anspach grumbles. He says,
"He's not here. He's at camp."

I shake my head. "Didn't he tell
you?" "Tell me what?" "What's
going on at that camp?"

"That—and he—are really none
of your business. Go home,
Jew boy." I feel a sucker punch right to the gut.

GRATEFUL
BENJY

Dear Pop, thank you
for teaching me to stand
up for myself and others.

Thank you for teaching
me right from wrong.
Thank you for always
listening even when
you may not want to.

Thank you for never
wanting me to be someone
I'm not. Thank you and Ma
for always letting me be me.

I know others aren't that lucky.
Boy, do I know.

THE LIGHT OF DARKNESS
THOMAS

"Where is your uniform?" Leader Klapprott asks.
"I'm not going to wear it."
"You must."

"No, it's against the law. Don't you know that?"
I have crossed the line and I know it.
A vein throbs in his forehead and spittle

forms at the edges of his mouth.
"There are consequences for disobedience,"
he says. "I know," I say. "I've seen it in the lake."

He hauls me by my collar up toward the lake
to a ramshackle shack that must not be rentable.
He thrusts open the dilapidated door and tosses

me in with such force that I stumble
and hit the earthen floor. Light slices
into the one room through gaps

in the wooden slat walls.
"You will stay here in isolation. You will
think about the dishonor you bring

to yourself, Camp Nordland, me, and even
Adolf Hitler. I had such high hopes for you."
"There's nothing you can do,

"Herr Direktor Klapprott,
to hurt me. Not really.
I have right on my side.

"Your days, Camp Nordland's days,
the Bund's days,
are numbered."

He kicks dirt at me,
but I don't care. He locks
the door on the outside.

But even in this darkness,
I can see more clearly than ever.

You are the one in darkness,
Klapprott. You are the one
in denial.

MIDNIGHT REFLECTION
THOMAS

You searched for me in the hallways, but I did not want to see you.
You tried to warn me, but I did not want to hear you.
You reached out to me, but I did not want to touch you.
Now at midnight, is it midnight? I sit alone at Nordland. In some shack.
The door is locked from the outside. The chain and padlock
clank against the wooden bolt. The sound blocks out the scurrying
of what I'm sure are furry creatures with red eyes.
I call out to you, Benjy. Can you hear me?

I SIT ON A RAGGED EDGE, LEGS DANGLING
THOMAS

I sit on a ragged edge, legs dangling,
overlooking a valley and mountain range.
Alone with my thoughts, a way out angling

This nightmare is real, loose ends hanging,
tying me into knots, must rearrange.
I sit on a ragged edge, legs dangling

Nordland is fake, Klapprott's words clanging
in my head. It's all wrong, radical, strange.
Alone with my thoughts, a way out angling.

The more I think about him, sneer mangling,
I know what I must do; he is deranged.
I sit on a ragged edge, legs dangling

Even in dirt, I must stand up, wrangling,
fight my way out, show everyone I've changed.
Alone with my thoughts, a way out's angling.

And you, Herr Klapprott, no longer tangling
with me, I'm getting out, with no exchange.
I sit on a ragged edge, legs dangling,
wresting my thoughts, a way out's angling.

I CAN FEEL IT
BENJY

Tommy needs me, I can feel it.
The way I can feel like it's going
to rain in my healed ribs.

I've never felt this before,
this tugging at me,
these whispers groping me.

My dreams, my nightmares
are full of Tommy. I see
him in chains in darkness.

How could his father allow him,
force him, to go back to Nordland?
I know how. He's in denial.

He refuses to believe.
We'll make him believe,
Tommy and I.

Tommy's in danger.
I can feel it.
Like he's caught

in a sheet of despair
in a veil of invisibility,
his bare feet on dirt floor.

I'M COMING

THOMAS/TOMMY

I don't know how long I've been in this shack.
It stinks of my pee.
I try to keep my mind active
by solving algebra equations in my head. I
taste blood in my mouth from biting
my cracked lips too hard. I try to summon
up saliva. My mouth has gone dry.
I keep hearing, "I'm coming." My
head throbs but I still hear, "I'm coming."

THAT NIGHT AT MY HOUSE
BENJY

I pretended I wasn't listening,
I pretended I didn't care.

One part of me now says,
why should I care?

The other part says,
because Tommy came to me for help.

I rack my brain trying to remember
all that Tommy told me that night at my house:

The main building
the fields
the tents, barracks, and cabins
and the lake.

I draw a map, but not to scale.
I don't know distances.

That night at my house,
I had a chance to make things right.

I botched it.
Now with the help

of the Minutemen,
I'll have power in both hands

inside the ring of Nordland.

MINUTEMEN ON A MISSION
BENJY

By the time I clamber into Pop's car,
I see Mr. Arno and three other
Minutemen. "There's strength in numbers,"
Mr. Arno says. "Let's go rescue your friend."

We drive through the city and through
dusty roads to get to Andover. The camp
gates are already familiar. Brass knuckles
bulge in the Minutemen pockets. We are
contenders today and we are ready to fight.
We may not wear satin trunks, and we may not
lace up our gloves, but we can still land a punch,
even if it's words we're throwing.

I TAKE OFF
BENJY

Is the Nordland fence electrified?
If I touch it, will I be a goner from the shock?

I already have an electric current running
through me, a buzzing, an energy

that propels me forward, no matter the risk.
I have to believe that Mr. Arno, Pop,

and the other Minutemen will keep
the camp sentries busy so I can

try to find Tommy. Pop hands me
a walkie-talkie. He says, "Signal me

when you find him." I nod and take off.
I pull out my map.

I spot the main building and its
NORDLAND sign. Only one problem:

There's a swarm of campers
stampeding toward me.

MEETING THE OPPOSITION
BENJY

Do I feint to the left?
Do I turn to the right?
Do I drop to one knee?

But the campers don't seem
to care about me. They

create a windstorm as they pass
me, the momentum causing me

to curl up. I protect my eyes
with my hands, nearly losing my map.

They rush to the gate, fists raised,
shouting in English and German.

What would they do if they knew
a Jew, a few Jews, were on the grounds?

MAP TO NOWHERE
BENJY

Just to the right of the main building
the graveled path should lead to the lake
and the barracks. I run and run until I get shin

splints and then I run some more.
I'm like a boxer running willy-nilly
in the ring, chased by something

I can't see, running toward something
I don't know. I don't know where
Tommy is.

If I were in trouble, where would
I be? I'd be hiding. But where?
In the woods?

Trying to find Tommy among
the evergreens would be like
trying to find a four-leaf clover

in Weequahic Park.
I can't imagine he'd be in his
barracks or tent, wherever

he'd been bunking with his
comrades. Too obvious.
So what's left?

Static buzzes from my
walkie-talkie. I can hear Mr. Arno
say, "We know what goes on here," and

someone saying, "Call the police!" Then
a Yiddish voice says, "Here's your police,"
and I hear metal clash against metal. More

static. Then, "Pop to Pup, Pop to Pup!
You'd better hurry! We can't keep them
much longer! Too many of them!"

CHANCE ENCOUNTER
BENJY

I don't know where to find him.
It's not like I have a crystal ball.

Finally, I see a camper, maybe ten years old,
alone by the lake. "Thomas, Thomas

Anspach? Have you seen him?" I say
in my best-ever German.

The camper looks me up and down,
"Ja," he says. "He's in the isolation cabin."

He smiles. "He's been bad."
"Where is this cabin?" I ask.

He points to the trees.
Why doesn't he ask me who I am

and what I am doing here?
"You a relative of his?" he says.

He thinks I'm German!
"Yeah, something like that," I say.

KNOCKDOWN
BENJY

I race around the lake.
I can't feel my feet anymore.
I'm sweating as if I've fought
ten rounds, maybe twelve,
in the ring. I can feel the sweat
running down my face, my chin,
my neck, my stomach. My face
must be red and I want to vomit.

But I don't have time for that.
I spot something between the trees,
a sort of shack. The door has
a chain lock. I start pounding
on the door. "Tommy, Tommy,
are you in there?"

A voice calls out, too weak
for me to be certain it's him.
I survey the shack. No windows.
How to get to him? I could slide
between the ropes if this were
a ring, but wooden slats?

Wait, one of them seems to be
loose. I kick at it, push all my
welterweight against the rotting
wood. It gives way and I crash
onto the dirt floor.

I pick myself up the way Pop
taught me to do after a knockdown,
like I'm made of rubber, all bouncy.
There in the corner is a huddled
mass. "Tommy, is that you?"

I inch over. The place smells
like the Newark subway station,
of piss and neglect. I kneel down.

"Tommy."

GOT HIM!
BENJY

"Pup to Pop! Pup to Pop!
Come in, Pop!" I let go of
the Talk button for a moment
to wipe sweat from my forehead.
"Found him!
A shack in the woods on the left
side of the lake."

Tommy says nothing. I don't think
he can. I wish I had thought
to bring a canteen or something.

We've got him, though.
We rescued Tommy.

THE SHACK
BENJY

One of the Minutemen picks the lock,
a skill he learned working for Longie Zwillman.
Pop picks up Tommy like a bundle of wood.

We run.

Mr. Arno's fingers pull through
the brass knuckles. The other Minutemen
do the same. Some of them hold clubs, too.

I know we're going to run into the sentries,
the campers too. I don't know how
we're going to outsmart the opposition.

We need another diversion. "There!"
I yell. In the field is a hay truck. "We
can commandeer it, at least to the gate!"

MAKE A RUN FOR IT
BENJY

Finding Tommy was like finding
a needle in a haystack. Now he's in the haystack,
resting comfortably, I hope. Mr. Arno's
driving the hay truck at breakneck speed
toward the gate. We rumble along the grass
with half the camp, all the camp, running
alongside us, behind us, yelling shouting,
"Get off our property!"
"You don't belong here!"
I expect the police to show up
any minute. I'm not too fond of them
since the Bund meeting.
Then I hear over the public-address system,
"Stop them! They've kidnapped
a camper!" Mr. Arno floors it
and before we know it, we've outpaced
the opposition. We're at the gate.
We transfer to the car
and take off like bank robbers,
only we're the good guys.

ON THE WAY HOME
BENJY

I have sore, searing thoughts
swirling in my head, asking how could Tommy
once believe in this bunk, the junk they poured
into his muddled brain. I know he sees it
now for the canker sore it really is.

WE STOP AT TOMMY'S HOUSE
BENJY

Tommy's coherent now,
he's had some water and some food.

We pull up in front of his house.
"I don't want to go in," he says.
"You've got to, son," Pop says.
"Benjy and I will help you."

Pop helps him out of the car
and up the front stairs. He
rings the bell. I'm holding
Tommy up. He's still
pretty weak.

Mr. Anspach answers the door
with Mrs. Anspach right behind
him. She gasps and covers her mouth.
She reaches for Tommy. "My boy," she cries.
I follow them into the parlor
where she clears a place on the sofa
for him to lie down. Pop
and Mr. Anspach enter the room.

"What has happened?" Mr. Anspach
asks Pop. "He got in trouble
for disobeying the uniform rules,
even though it's against the law to wear them," I say.
"He was locked up
in an isolation cabin, no food or water."

Mrs. Anspach rushes in with a pot of tea.
She holds Tommy's head while she forces
him to take some sips.

"This cannot be so," Mr. Anspach says.
"It's true," Tommy murmurs. "I tried . . .
I tried to tell you. You didn't want to listen."

Mr. Anspach looks at Pop, one adult
to another. Pop says, "It's true, all right.
Just look at this poor boy."

By the time Pop and I leave, Tommy is asleep
in his own bed and Mr. Anspach
is shaking his head and pouring another beer,
muttering something about Jewish propaganda.

SKIN

TOMMY

The skin I was in doesn't suit me anymore—
No khakis, marching, or salutes

The skin I was in proved only a veneer
like the cheap, chipped counter at Sol's deli

The skin I was in buttoned me up tight,
my heart, my lungs, my lips, my thoughts

The skin I was in has molted like a snake's.
I scrub until stars and stripes shine bright.

MOTHER'S TEA
TOMMY

"Gerhard, look what's been done to him!"
"Gerhard, he is your son!"
"Gerhard, Rudi is dead. Tommy is alive.
Barely."

Mother makes me some tea,
because she knows I like
it with six sugar cubes
when I'm sick.

She sits on the side of the bed
and puts the back of her hand
against my forehead.

"Tell me everything,"
she says, cradling my head
in her arms.

I STILL REFUSE
TOMMY

Father, I obeyed you before when you wanted me
to return to Nordland. I won't go back this time.

> You'll do what I say as long as
> you live under my roof.

You don't know what goes on there.
It's all a front, all a façade.

> What do you know?
> You're just a child.

I may be a teenager, but you
didn't raise me to be stupid.
Do you want me to tell you
about how I was locked up?
How the camp director threw me
into this shack because I refused
to disobey the law?

> You must have done something wrong.

It's illegal in New Jersey, Father,
to wear Nazi uniforms.

> (He shrugs.)

Oh, Father, open your eyes!
Read a real newspaper!
Listen to real news!
There's going to be war!
Worse than the Great War!
Worse than you or I could ever imagine!

HERE'S THE DEAL
TOMMY

If you make me go back, Father,
I'll keep running away
and I won't come back here.
I'll go somewhere else.
You'll never find me.
You'll be as dead to me
as Rudi is to you.

If you make me go back, Father,
I'll find a way to stay in touch
with Mother but never with you.
I won't have a father
and you won't have a son.

Hitler's not the only one
who can make ultimatums.

THE DECISION
TOMMY

You have to go back, Father says,
I've paid for your summer
and for our cabin.

You have to go back, Father says,
I have a reputation to uphold.

You have to go back, Father says.

Then the decision is made, I say.
I'll pack my things and leave.

I throw my clothes into a paper bag
and let the back door bang behind me.

I HIT THE STREETS
TOMMY

Father will know if I go to Benjy's.
I walk around Weequahic,
keeping to myself until it's time
to meet Benjy at Sol's.
"Staying with Mr. Arno is a good idea,
right?" I ask, as Benjy hands me
the address. I'm proud of myself
for thinking of Mr. Arno. No one
can hurt me with him around
and Father would never think
of looking for me with a Minuteman.

"Still," I say, "I worry about my mother
and how she'll worry about me."
Benjy buys me a soda, but I can't drink it.
"Maybe I should send you
to my grandma."

"I'll still have to show up for school
in September," I say. "I need to talk
to my mother."

MY BUBBE TO THE RESCUE
BENJY

Ma talks to Tommy's mother.
Ma talks to Grandma.
But it's my bubbe who comes to the rescue.

At her house, she says to Mrs. Anspach,
"You're always welcome."
She gestures to the empty
parlor full of framed family photos
and doily-covered surfaces.
"I got plenty of space
and I like people to talk to.
And maybe this means I'll see
my grandson more often!"

She pinches my cheek.
"And you know," she continues,
"the high school is only a spit away."
I love my grandma!

SHADOWS
TOMMY

I can lose myself in Superman comics,
slurp down an ice-cream soda,
but I can't forget Nordland.

I still see shadows of swastikas,
hear *Sieg Heil!* salutes, taste
the bitterness of hatred.

But I'm on safe ground now,
growing my hair longer,
and hanging out with Benjy.

I just wish I could wake up
in my own room, the sun streaming in,
the garbage cans banging into each other.

If only I were bigger
If only I were stronger
If only I were older
Maybe Father would listen to me.

MONKEY IN THE MIDDLE
BENJY
August 22, 1939

"Reich and Soviet Agree on No-War Pact"
—United Press, August 22, 1939

Imagine this:
In the boxing ring of Europe,
Hitler's Germany in black trunks
and Stalin's Soviet Union in red trunks
put up their dukes, looking like
they're going to throw serious blows.
But instead they unlace their gloves
and shake hands in the middle of the ring.

In the middle of the ring
is Poland, that country that
lies between Germany and the Soviet Union.
Hitler looks at Poland.
Stalin looks at Poland.
Then they look at each other
and smirk. They're about to play
monkey in the middle,
while the rest of the world
looks on from the spectator seats.

IT'S STARTING
TOMMY
August 22, 1939

It won't be long now. I imagine saying to Father.
Front-page headlines are full of
war!
German guns sixteen feet long
with plenty of firepower
roll toward Poland, Father.

I want to thrust the paper
in front of your face,
bend your head to the printed letters.
It's real!
Will you believe me now?

GRANDMA TRIES TO REPAIR THE WORLD
BENJY
August 27, 1939

Bubbe carries a chocolate-frosted
layer cake with sixteen flaming candles
into her dining room.

"You've outdone yourself, Mama,"
Pop says to Bubbe as he takes
his third slice of the birthday cake.

"You are an excellent baker,"
Mrs. Puterman," Tommy's mother says.
"You must give me the recipe."

"What recipe?" Bubbe asks. "A little
of this, a little of that." She pinches
my cheek and then Tommy's.
"And a lot of love."

SOMEONE'S MISSING
TOMMY

I keep looking at the front door,
waiting for Father to come
to his senses, to come
to the door and apologize to me.

I keep looking at the front door,
hoping we can be a family again
and put Nordland and Nazism
out of our lives for good.

I keep looking at the front door
until Mother turns my head away
and says, "Eat your cake."

THE WORLD SPINS TO WAR!
BENJY
August 30, 1939

Newspaper headlines are screaming,
streaming, war is coming:
Hitler's given an ultimatum to Poland
        to return land lost in the last war.
Poland calls up its military reserves!

IT'S DONE
TOMMY
September 1, 1939

Done!
Nordland's lost its license
to sell liquor on camp grounds.

Done!
German tanks thunder through
fields and cobblestoned streets
of western Poland.

While New Jersey makes its way
to being Nazi-free,
the world has a long way to go.

WAR!

BENJY AND TOMMY
September 2, 1939

"Poland Bombed"
"Warsaw [Poland] Calls for Britain's Aid" —*Paterson Evening News*,
$\qquad\qquad\qquad\qquad\qquad\qquad$ September 1, 1939

Ladies and gentlemen,
the fight of the century

> In this corner, Nazi Germany and pals
> Italy and the Soviet Union.
> In the opposite corner, Poland.

Both sides lace up their gloves
Hitler throws an explosive
Fog and smoke everywhere

> Is Poland still standing?

To help Poland,
England, France, and Canada
climb over the ropes,
declarations of war tucked
into their gloves.

I NEED TO TALK TO FATHER
TOMMY
September 5, 1939

I want to come home, sleep in my own room,
although Grandma Puterman is like my own Oma,
and I am grateful for her care.

I need to talk to Father.
I need to see if he's ready to hear
the truth now that there's war
and not just rumors of it.

Mother arranges the visit.
I ring the doorbell
and my stomach
is getting pummeled
from the inside.

A VISIT WITH FATHER
TOMMY

Father answers the door
and gestures toward the parlor.

Not a beer in sight. No bottle
of schnapps on the shelf above the radio.

"I haven't had a drink since you left,"
he says. "Maybe I mean more to you

than you thought," I say. He nods
and offers me a glass of apple juice,

pours a glass for himself.
"I've had plenty of time to think

in the last few weeks," he says. "But
I cannot change my ways. I cannot

change what I believe in. I understand
you feel differently." My stomach

pulls in like I've been punched hard.
I expected my father to be reasonable.

He says, "Since you are my son, and under age,
I will allow you to live here still.

I will tolerate your lack of allegiance to Germany."
I gulp the apple juice because I don't know

what else to do. I *am* his son, I *am* under age.
But just wait, Father, just wait till I'm eighteen.

Mother comes through
the door and asks, "All is set right, *ja*?"

IT'S CLEAR TO ME
TOMMY

Mother must have forced Father
into this reconciliation. But is it
one? Feels more like a conspiracy.

How can I say no to my mother,
who stands behind Father,
her hands on his shoulders,

nodding to me to say yes
when Father invites me to stay?

A FAMILY AGAIN?
TOMMY

Father drops the Meerschaum pipe
he was tamping. The tone of his voice
changes, softens to a near whisper.

"For me, Nordland was a way
back. A place that reminded
me of home and when I was young."

I bite my tongue. I know from
experience it does no good
to speak my mind. My opinions

bounce off Father's deflection shields.
Father picks up his pipe
and opens the tobacco pouch.

He stuffs his pipe and gets a good smoke
going. Mother comes into the parlor
to announce sauerbraten for dinner.

Sauerbraten. Can't we just call it braised beef?

IN THE CAFETERIA
BENJY AND TOMMY

How's it going at home?

> Like walking on shards of glass
> all the time. Never know
> when something Father says
> or I say will cut the other.
> So we say nothing.

Can you stick it out?

> If I were old enough,
> I'd enlist in the Canadian
> Royal Air Force.

I'd go with you,
if we were old enough.

> The minute I turn eighteen,
> I'm off to Canada.

PART III:

THE DOOR CLOSES, 1940-1941

THESE ARE TRYING TIMES
BENJY

President Roosevelt wants to remain our president. He's the first president who wants to serve more than two terms. It's unheard of! But Pop says we need him to stay right where he is, because there's war all around us, and though he's told us we'll stay out of it, I'm not so sure.

Grandma wrings her hands and shakes her head. She doesn't want another war. I say, Grandma, no one wants another war. But when you've got characters like Hitler and Stalin, well, they're not going to play tiddlywinks.

Meanwhile, at the synagogue we always pray for our relatives in Germany, Austria, and now Poland. We pray they'll be able to escape. That someone will help rescue them and bring them somewhere safe. Wherever that may be.

And yet I keep asking myself, am I doing enough? Will I look back at this time in my later years and regret not having done my part?

REFUGEES
BENJY

If we all sent invitations to cousins overseas,
then maybe they'd muster the courage to leave
so we could crush Hitler and Stalin.

If we all gathered in warmer seas
and guided our refugees to the Azores and Spain,
then maybe they could wait out their visas
for American destinations.

If we all decided
the eagles of the great European houses
were more like our bald eagle
with no orb, no crown
no false promises.
If all the eagles of the Third Reich were
to swear allegiance
to the red, white, and blue,
and really mean it,
then maybe we'd have the chance we need
to preserve the democracy of our Founding Fathers
from swamp to coastline.

THE WORLD NEEDS A BOWL OF BUBBE'S SOUP
BENJY

Bubbe, my grandma, places a bowl of her vegetable soup
in front of me. Smack dab in the middle
is a knee bone—my favorite.
My mouth waters just looking
at the globules of luscious fat on the bone.
"The fat gives so much flavor," she says.
"The fat and the bones."

I love my grandma and her soft skin
and flowered dresses, her tight gray curls
and even the brown spots on her gnarled hands.

I love her accent and how many times
she can say "oy" in one sentence.

I thank G-d that she and Zayde left
Europe before the first war to come
to America and resettle their dreams.

Had they stayed in Poland, they could now
be in Hitler's clutches. Bubbe prays
for her family still there. But swastika
tentacles have long reach. Hitler wants Europe.
He wants Britain. He wants America.
May G-d have mercy on us all.

MYTHOLOGY AND REALITY
BENJY
April 9, 1940

We're learning about Roman, Greek, and Norse
mythology. Mrs. Hamilton has us reading
the pantheon of deities and I think about Thor,
the Norse god of thunder.

Germany invaded Norway today, and Denmark, too.
Odin, the Norse god of war, is having his way.
Hitler is a shape-shifter, taking on whatever appearance
he wants. Behind his mask is Loki, the trickster god.
He's not done yet.

GOOD THING TOMMY'S NO LONGER AT NORDLAND

BENJY AND TOMMY
May 10, 1940

"What do you think would have happened,"
I ask Tommy, "if you had stayed at Camp Nordland?"

> "We'd be loading real guns.
> We'd be stepping up the drilling.
> We'd be celebrating Nazi victories
> > invading Holland
> > invading Belgium
> > invading Luxembourg."

THE MAP OF EUROPE
BENJY AND TOMMY

We'll soon be running out of fingers
to count all the countries now involved.
Nazi Germany has dropped bombs on France today, too.

One-two-three-four
Hitler's marching west for more

Five-six-seven-eight
Hitler's guns will decimate

The red-and-black blotch of Nazi Germany

spreads like spilled ink all over the map of Europe.

NOTHING RILES FATHER
TOMMY

Nazi Germany is taking over
Western Europe while Father
reads his newspaper and listens to Wagner.

Nazi Germany spreads to the west
and Father goes out to celebrate
at the Turnverein Hall.

We live in the same house
but on different continents.

WE NEED TO DO SOMETHING NOW
BENJY

Now is not the time to enlist.
We're still too young.

Now is not the time for the Minutekids.
The Bund's been quiet.

Now is not the time to join
Junior ROTC, military training at school.
It takes too long. But there's always
the Canadian Royal Air Force! Canada's
in the fight along with Great Britain.

Tommy and I rifle through our
superhero comic books for inspiration.

I'VE GOT IT!
BENJY

I make plans to talk to Mr. Schneider,
head of phys ed.

"Come with me," I say to Tommy,
and I grab him by the arm. I drag
him through the hallways

until we enter the gym. "Mr.
Schneider," I say, "I know we don't
have a boxing team, but I wonder

if we could raise funds
for the war, you know, for England,
a friend of the United States

that's been bravely facing
the nightly barrage of Nazi bombs,
and for refugees by arranging

a series of boxing matches. I know
a few of the Minutemen, and I'll bet
they'd be willing to help,

and then maybe Tommy and I
could go into the ring against
each other, too."

Before I can blink, Mr. Schneider
shleps us to the principal's office.
Oy, I'm thinking, Benjy, you've

done it now. But Mr. Schneider
actually likes the idea, and so does
Mr. Herzog, the principal.

I go home and Pop likes the idea
too. "I'll talk to the guys," he says.
"We'll be able to match up some

pretty good fights." He pats me
on the back, and I'm kvelling with pride.
Even Tommy says, "Good one, Benjy boy!"

WE PRACTICE
BENJY AND TOMMY

Pop takes us to Joe's downtown,
where the Minutemen keep
in shape. I put on my headgear
and gloves, getting ready to rumble.

> "How did I let you talk me into this?
> I don't know how to box."

"There's nothing to it."
I help with his gear
"Start with this punching bag."
He packs a wallop.

> "Hey, I might be good at this!
> Teach me something else!"

I show him how to dance,
how to duck, how to protect,
how to jab, punch, land
an uppercut.

> "You've got some fancy footwork!"
> I'm going to like this.

We spend hours in the gym,
dancing and ducking,
punching and pretending
to pulverize. Pop buys us
each a Coke when we're done.

"What a match
people are going to see!"

Two kids from Weequahic!

"Funny how we never learned boxing
at Nordland. Not military enough, I guess."

"You're doing it now!"

"So are you!"

LET'S RUMBLE!
BENJY

Ladies and Gentlemen, what a great night
for a great cause! Help the refugees flee Europe!

In our first event, we have
Benjy "The Kid" Puterman, in blue trunks,
vs Tommy "The Avenger" Anspach in white trunks.
There's the bell, and they're off.
Puterman dances in and out,
ducking Anspach's jabs.
Puterman lobs an uppercut to the chin
and Anspach lowers to the canvas.
Wait, no, he gets up.
But Puterman's at him again,
pummels the stomach
like a bongo drum
moving across the floor
until Anspach tangles in the ropes.
The bell sounds, and it's the end
of the first round, ladies and gents.

The bell rings, and both contenders
jump to the center of the ring.
Anspach lands a punch to the gut
that sends Puterman reeling
to the corner. But The Kid rebounds
and comes at The Avenger with
vengeance. He delivers
a double left hook, ducks a counterpunch.
The Avenger goes for a clinch,
but the referee breaks them apart.

Both contenders grin. They're both
winners, ladies and gents! Too bad
Anspach's mom and dad aren't here
to witness the mutual victory!

In the final exhibition round of our first event,
The Kid and Avenger go at it one last time.
Puterman does his signature dance,
not letting Anspach land anything.
Oh! Puterman throws a punch,
and another, and another!
Anspach's down, folks, one.
two, three, four, five. He tries
to get up. What's this? Puterman
helps him up and they both
raise their gloves to the air!
Great job, boys!

And now for tonight's main event:
Nat Arno in red trunks
vs Harry "The Obliterator" Puterman in gold.
Arno makes the first move and lands
a one-two with an uppercut followed
by a left hook. These are professionals,
folks. Puterman counters with a left hook
of his own with great precision, but
it bounces off Arno like
a pebble across water. Arno feints a jab
but Puterman's too smart to let that
make him react. That's the bell,
and the end of Round 1.

Folks, we've raised thirty-five thousand dollars tonight
to help the refugees. Our biggest donor

of the night is longtime Newark
supporter, no matter what anyone says,
Longie Zwillman! Thanks, Longie!

And now back to the fight for Round Two.
Arno and Puterman are at it again. Arno's
the more technical of the two, but Puterman's
got more energy. He bobs and weaves
making Arno dizzy. Then Puterman
lands a jab, follows with an uppercut,
sends Arno into a spin to the floor.
The referee counts: one, two, three, four, five!
And Arno's up, shaking his head. He throws
a punch to the chest, but Puterman deflects
and lands another uppercut. Again, Arno
spins to the ground for a three-count.
Round Two is over!

Thanks go to Weequahic High
and Principal Herzog for the use
of the gym for tonight's exhibition!
We can always count on Newark
for support, right, folks!

And there's the bell for the final round.
Puterman starts with a hook and a jab.
Arno counters with a rabbit punch
behind the head, drawing Puterman
into a clinch. The referee says, "Stop!"
and separates them. Puterman dances
his bob and weave around Arno and
lands a cross from the left. He feints a punch.
Arno counters but hits
the air. Puterman delivers a hook

and his uppercut and Arno is down
for the count. It's over, folks!
Puterman has KO'd Arno!
It's been a helluva night for Newark boxing!
It's been a helluva night for Newark!
It's been a helluva night to fight for refugees!

AFTER THE FIGHTS
BENJY AND TOMMY

We all go out for ice cream.
I think I gave Tommy a black eye!
But he's feeling no pain
as our spoons clink against each other
in the metal bowl that holds
our banana split.

Pop and Ma sit drinking coffee. Mr. Arno
swaggers up to us. He says, "If
we ever need younger Minutemen,
you two are the first I'd recruit."

FRANCE KO'D

BENJY

June 22, 1940

France gave it all she had.
But once she knelt down
on one knee, the fight's over.

Hitler demands her surrender.
Beaten, bruised, and bloody,
France has no choice.

She's carried out of the ring.

Who's next to step onto the canvas?
Britain steps forward. But Hitler
drops a bomb. Again and again.

Britain's going to have to do
some pretty fancy footwork
and land those counterpunches
to avoid a knockout.

PREPARING FOR ANOTHER KNOCKDOWN
TOMMY

I want to see how long
it will take for the authorities
to deliver a fatal blow
to Camp Nordland.

I read the papers every day
to find news. Despite the number
of knockdowns, Nordland hasn't been
knocked out. Yet. But maybe now
is the time, especially since
Leader Kuhn,
I should say,
former Leader Kuhn,
is still in jail.

DOWN FOR THE COUNT
TOMMY
July 4, 1940

"Not guilty!" three Bund leaders insist
as they're brought
before a Sussex County hearing.

"Not guilty!" three Bund leaders persist.
"We did not violate the anti-uniform law."

"Not guilty!" three Bund leaders enlist
the aid of their lawyers to make bail
of a thousand dollars each. But the money
comes in too late.

"Not guilty!" three Bund leaders' pleas dismissed
as they're locked up in jail.

ANOTHER KNOCKOUT CLOSER TO HOME
TOMMY
September 12, 1940

The windows rattle to the point of shattering.
The shingles of the roof fall to the ground.
We run out into the night.
Rumbling like the end of the world—
someone says it's the Hercules Powder plant
by Camp Nordland.
Is it the act of Nazis in New Jersey?

NOT IN THE PLAYBOOK
TOMMY
September 13, 1940

Tear up the songbooks!
Take down the swastika!
Drain the illegal beer kegs!
Expose Nordland for what it is.

Kick down the cabin doors.
Riffle through the cupboard shelves.
Find the evidence, boys!
English or German!

What have we here?
A photo of Hitler
A uniform with cross-body leather belt
A swastika-marked rifle with telescopic sight
Reams of antisemitic rhetoric
Haul this evidence and take these
Nazis into custody.

THE COLORS OF WAR
BENJY AND TOMMY
September 28, 1940

"The British beat back powerful German air attacks today as
Nazis described [yesterday's] triple alliance among Germany, Italy and
Japan as a 'red light' cautioning Russia as well as the United States
against attempting to interfere in the wars with Great Britain and
China."   —*Herald-News* (Passaic, NJ), September 28, 1940

We spread out a map
on the floor of my bedroom.

     We use thumbtacks
     to track the war in Europe.

We use red and black
to mark the assaults

     of Germany and Italy.
     We use blue to mark

the moves of Britain and France.
What color will we use

     to route Japan's attacks
     in Asia and the Pacific?

Hitler is bringing Japan's Emperor Hirohito
into his brotherhood of aggression

wanting Japan to engage
in an attack on England.

We throw all the thumbtacks
into the air.

ON THE ROPES
TOMMY

If Father has taught me one thing,
it's that we become our choices.
Each yes and no makes us lean
into darkness or light
into empty or full.
But there's an invisible continuum
along the spectrum of possible
between salty and sweet.
In the middle sit all the questions
that teeter for the right responses.

IT'S OFFICIAL
TOMMY
May 31, 1941

One by one
a dozen members of the American Legion approached.

Low fog hovered above the grasses
like a net to protect the growth.

"By order of the New Jersey Attorney General,"
the Sussex County Sheriff said, "this is a raid."

The state unanimously voted
to repeal Nordland's charter,
take it back
cancel it
revoke it
withdraw it.

Camp Nordland will stand abandoned.
Weeds will overgrow the sign
and choke the entrance.

Tent flaps will tatter in the wind.
Cobwebs will drape the cabins.

Camp Nordland will become a ghost,
but I'll bet the stench of beer

will remain strong but stale
and the sound of marching boots

will still beat to the rhythm
of a new world order bottled in fantasy.

Here on these grounds
the earth will always rumble
and bear witness to Camp Nordland.

KNOCK ME OUT!
BENJY
June 22, 1941

Hitler's given Stalin a sly one-two punch
to the gut. He doesn't fight a clean fight.

He's invaded the Soviet Union,
reneged on their pact. He's going
for the title shot: Emperor of the World.

WE'RE GRADUATES NOW
BENJY AND TOMMY
June 1941

Diplomas in hand,
our paths paved
to college
in September!

      I, Tommy to the Newark College of Engineering.

I, Benjy to Rutgers here in the city,
but it will be hard to stay focused

      on our studies
      with the world at war.

Almost the world—
America's not in it yet

      and our eyes on the Royal Air Force.

A BLESSING FOR BENJY
TOMMY

I thank you, my oldest friend,
for never giving up on me.
Subtle
and delicate do not define you—
or me—you pummeled your well-worn
fists in my face, unraveling the threads
of shadow and night. It's day again
and I feel alive as I walk beside you
on Peshine Avenue and eat a kosher pickle
from Sol's once more.

THE LAST TIME AT NORDLAND
TOMMY
August 1941

Nordland—a dream, a nightmare,
a prelude to war.
The guns
The salutes
The flags
The allegiance to Hitler

I'm ready to move beyond
this stalemate with Father
and fly.

TWO CONTENDERS ENTER THE BOXING RING
BENJY AND TOMMY

We're off to Canada
to join its air force.
We'll learn how to fly planes
and drop bombs
against Germany.

We're off to face the enemy!

EPILOGUE

CAMP NORDLAND officially closed on June 6, 1941, with the revocation of its charter. It was sold to 217 individual members of the Bund. However, the federal government soon seized control. In June 1944, a local real estate dealer purchased the property for private ownership. The Township of Andover acquired the property and renamed it Hillside Park. At least one of the Nordland buildings remains.

Bund leader **FRITZ KUHN** lost his American citizenship in 1943 while imprisoned at Sing Sing federal prison in Ossining, New York. He was deported to Germany in 1945 and worked for two years as an industrial chemist. But German authorities decided to try him under the country's postwar de-Nazification laws. While awaiting trial, he managed to escape but was found and returned to prison. He was released shortly before his death in 1951.

Camp director and New Jersey Bund leader **AUGUST KLAPPROTT** faced federal charges of conspiracy against the United States. He was indicted in 1942. The decision was upheld in the court of appeals in 1944. He remained in prison until 1945 and lost his American citizenship. He died in South Carolina at the age of ninety-six.

The **GERMAN-AMERICAN BUND** dissolved after its top members voted to disband at a final meeting on December 16, 1941.

Representative **SAMUEL DICKSTEIN** (NY) resigned from Congress in 1945. He then served as a justice for the New York State Supreme Court until his death in 1954.

The need for the **NEWARK MINUTEMEN** diminished as the Bund lost its power and World War II intensified. **NAT ARNO** joined the army and eventually moved to California, where he died in 1973.

Nazi swastikas fly high on July 18, 1937, at the opening of Camp Nordland in rural Andover, New Jersey.

German-American Bund members fill New York City's Madison Square Garden at a rally in January 1939.

Former boxer Nat Arno (center with cigar) and his group of anti-Nazi vigilantes, the Newark Minutemen, helped to protect the Jews of New Jersey.

AUTHOR'S NOTE

My interest in New Jersey's Camp Nordland began around 2003 when I read Warren Grover's *Nazis in Newark*. I began to find newspaper articles but my research started in earnest in the summer of 2014 when I conducted research at the Jewish Historical Society of Greater MetroWest in Whippany, New Jersey, and trekked to Andover to meet with a representative of the town's historical society. There was only one piece of documentation. It seemed like Andover wanted to forget that part of its past. I stood on the grounds of the former Camp Nordland and could feel the heavy stomps in the ground itself.

In *Facing the Enemy*, I have combined two fictional characters—Benjy Puterman and Tommy Anspach—and their families, with references to real-life characters who shaped the destiny of Camp Nordland: Bund leader Fritz Kuhn, camp director August Klapprott, US House of Representatives Samuel Dickstein (Democrat, NY), Newark Minutemen leader Nat Arno, and Newark's lovable Jewish gangster, Longie Zwillman.

Readers might be wondering where else the German-American Bund established youth camps. The number of these camps varies based on the source, but these are the ones I've come across in my research:

Camp Bergwald, Bloomingdale, NJ
Camp Eichenfeld, near Pontiac, MI
Camp Highland, Windham, NY
Camp Hindenburg/Camp Carl Schurz, Grafton, WI
Camp Siegfried, Yaphank, NY, on Long Island
Camp Sutter, near Los Angeles, CA
Deutschhorst Country Club, near Sellersville, PA

Other camp locations, according to the House Un-American Activities Committee:

Buffalo, NY
Cleveland, OH
Oakland, CA
Portland, OR
San Diego, CA
Schenectady, NY
Seattle, WA
Spokane, WA
St. Louis, MO

ACKNOWLEDGMENTS

Several writers encouraged me to create this work about Nazis and a youth camp in my own state of New Jersey. I owe a debt of gratitude to Shirley Reva Vernick and to members of the Amherst Writers & Artists "Deep-Enders" workshop—Susan "Deepam" Wadds, Laurie Elmquist, Mathilda-Anne Florence, Julian Gunn, Allison Hannah, and Kari Jones for their careful listening and imaginative suggestions.

I also must thank my longtime poetry mentor, Matthew Lippman, for his insistence on strong imagery and generating content with poetic form. I thank, too, Jill Hershorin, archivist for the Jewish Historical Society of Greater MetroWest, for her helpful assistance in locating materials and for connecting me to Warren Grover, author of *Nazis in Newark*, whom I thank for his careful review of the manuscript for historical accuracy.

I am grateful to my agent, Emelie Burl of the Susan Schulman Literary Agency, LLC, for her encouragement, meticulous reading, and suggestions. To Carolyn P. Yoder, editor extraordinaire, I give many and most humble thanks for the idea for the book and her insistence on high quality.

GLOSSARY

ARYAN: A racial designation constructed by Nazi Germany to demonstrate superiority over other "races." Appropriated from an ancient group of people in northern India.

AUF WIEDERSEHEN: German for *goodbye*, literally "until we see each other again."

BRATWURST: A German pork sausage.

BUBBE: Yiddish for *grandma*.

BUND: An alliance or organization, specifically the German-American Bund, a pro-Nazi group established in America in 1937.

CHAROSES: A mixture of chopped walnuts, apples, and wine served at the Passover holiday dinner to signify the mortar Hebrews were forced to use while enslaved in ancient Egypt.

"DEUTSCHLAND ÜBER ALLES": The German national anthem during Hitler's reign, literally "Germany above all."

DIRNDL: A gathered skirt made popular in the mountains of Austria.

EDELWEISS: A flowering plant that grows in the Alps.

FASCHING: The Germanic version of Mardi Gras or Carnival, a religious celebration before the beginning of Lent.

FÜHRER: German for *leader.*

FUSSBALL: German for *soccer,* literally "foot ball."

HANUKKAH: Jewish "Festival of Lights" to commemorate the victory of the Maccabee revolt against the Seleucids and the miracle of a tiny bit of oil lasting eight days, which enabled the rededication of the Temple in Jerusalem.

HUMMEL: Figurines of children, designed by German Catholic nun Sister Maria Innocentia Hummel.

KO: Boxing term meaning *knock out.*

KRISTALLNACHT: "Night of the Broken Glass," a two-day act of vandalism on November 9–10, 1938, in Germany and Austria against Jewish homes, businesses, and places of worship.

LEDERHOSEN: Leather shorts usually worn with suspenders in the Bavarian region of Germany.

LOX: Brined or cured salmon, from the Yiddish for *salmon,* "laks."

MACCABEES: Usually refers to Judas Maccabee and his brothers, Jewish warriors who defeated the Seleucids and rededicated the Second Temple of Jerusalem in the second century BCE.

"MA'OZ TSUR": "Rock of Ages," a song sung in either Hebrew or Yiddish on the Jewish holiday of Hanukkah.

MEIN KAMPF: A book written by Adolf Hitler while imprisoned during the 1920s. The title means *My Struggle.*

MESHUGANAH: Yiddish for *crazy.*

MEZUZAH: An ornamental casing with a daily Torah prayer inside that is nailed to a doorjamb to bless a Jewish building or home.

MISHIGAS: Yiddish for *craziness*.

POGROM: The Russian word for an attack against the Jews.

PROST: A German drinking expression, literally *cheers*.

REICH: German for *empire*.

SAUERBRATEN: German pot roast.

SCHNITZEL: A thin, fried pork or veal cutlet.

SEDER: Ceremonial dinner served on the first and second evening of Passover to commemorate the Jewish exodus from Egypt.

SHMALTZ: Yiddish for *chicken fat*.

SHUL: Yiddish for *synagogue*.

SIEG HEIL: A salute used in Nazi Germany to demonstrate allegiance to Adolf Hitler.

SPAETZLE: A kind of egg noodle usually served as a side dish with gravy.

SUDETENLAND: A mountainous region in northern Czechoslovakia that was seized by Nazi Germany.

SWASTIKA: A cross symbol found in many different and ancient cultures, most associated with Adolf Hitler and his followers.

TACHLIS: Yiddish for the *unvarnished truth*.

TEUTONIC: Relating to ancient Germanic peoples.

TIKKUN OLAM: A Hebrew term for the Jewish value of social justice, literally *repairing the world*.

TURNVEREIN: German for *athletic club*.

VALHALLA: A mythical ancient Nordic hall for slain warriors.

VALKYRIES: Figures from Nordic mythology who guide fallen soldiers to their final destinations, including Valhalla.

WEISSWURST: A German white sausage of minced veal and pork, literally *white sausage*.

WILLKOMMEN: German for *welcome*.

YIDDISH: A language spoken by Jews of central and eastern Europe that is mostly derived from German but mixed with Hebrew and some Slavic words.

YOM KIPPUR: The Jewish High Holy Day of Atonement.

ZAYDE: Yiddish for *grandfather*.

TIMELINE OF EVENTS

1933

Jan. 30   President Paul von Hindenburg appoints Adolf Hitler, leader of the National Socialist (Nazi) Party in Germany, to the position of chancellor.

Mar. 4   Franklin Delano Roosevelt begins his first term as president of the United States.

Apr.   Germany sanctions the establishment of a Nazi organization in America.

Apr. 16   Called the Friends of New Germany, the local Newark chapter holds its first meeting at the city's German social club meeting hall, the Schwabenhalle. The organization advertises meetings and distributes antisemitic propaganda.

Oct. 18   Newark mobster Arnold "Longie" Zwillman publicly opposes the Friends of New Germany with his Third Ward gang at the Schwabenhalle.

1934

Feb. 4   A Jewish newspaper reports on an anti-Nazi group that has emerged in Newark under the leadership of a former professional boxer, Nat Arno, born Sidney Nathaniel Abramowitz, with the support of Longie

Zwillman, from the Jewish War Veterans
Post 34 and the Young Men's Hebrew Club.

Aug. 2   Hitler becomes Führer (leader) upon the death of
Germany's president, von Hindenburg.

1935

Feb.   Rep. Samuel Dickstein (D-NY) and Rep. John William
McCormack (D-MA) release the findings of their
committee's study of the Friends of New Germany,
stating that Nazi Germany's government provided
propaganda for distribution in the United States.

Dec. 31   Friends of New Germany dissolves.

1936

Mar. 19   Fritz Kuhn is elected as Führer of the
German-American Bund, an organization to take
the place of Friends of New Germany.

1937

Feb.   Kuhn attends first recorded Bund meeting in
Irvington, NJ.

Mar.   Camp Nordland incorporates with August Klapprott,
New Jersey Bund leader, as its registered agent.

July 18   Camp Nordland opens; Kuhn and Klapprott give
speeches; Italian-Americans join.

July 25	Two thousand people attend the camp's second weekend; Klapprott says he would welcome a federal investigation.
July 26	Rep. Dickstein names forty-six Nazi propagandists before Congress; thirty New Jersey post commanders of the American Legion, Veterans of Foreign Wars, Jewish War Veterans, Irish Veterans, and the Order of the Purple Heart meet in Newark. They pass a resolution condemning the Bund for preaching Nazism and racial hatred. They also press for state and federal investigations of Camp Nordland.
Aug. 3	Rep. Samuel Dickstein (D-NY) names New Jersey Nazi propagandists before Congress.
Aug. 8	Newark's anti-Nazi vigilante group, the Minutemen, led by Jewish former boxer Nat Arno, plans to attack the camp without weapons. Nordland authorities hear about it and instead, the camp proclaims the day as Youth Sports Day.
Aug. 18	US government agents begin "sniffing around" Camp Nordland and other camps to determine subversive activities.

1938

Apr. 12	Nazi Germany occupies Austria to "merge" German people.
May 26	US House Resolution 282 (the "Dies Resolution") to authorize the formation of the House Committee to Investigate Un-American Activities passes with an overwhelming majority.

July 1	The town of Andover, New Jersey, insists Camp Nordland pay a $500 shooting gallery license fee.
July 6–15	Organized by President Franklin Roosevelt, the Evian Conference in Evian, France, takes place to discuss the situation of Jewish refugees. The United States refuses to alter its immigration laws to allow in refugees.
Sept. 16	A Bund meeting in Elizabeth, New Jersey, stops when thousands of protesters prevent Bund members from entering the meeting venue.
Sept. 30	Germany regains possession of the Sudetenland, German land given to Czechoslovakia at the end of World War I.
Oct. 2	Kuhn gives a talk in Union City, New Jersey. More than 1,000 protesters riot and throw bricks.
Oct. 10	Violence erupts at a Bund meeting at the New Milford, New Jersey, home of a Bund leader and his wife.
Nov. 9–10	A two-day riot of violence erupts throughout Germany and Austria that results in the arrests of thousands of Jewish men and boys, desecration of synagogues, and vandalism of Jewish homes and businesses. It's called "Night of the Broken Glass," or *Kristallnacht*.

1939

Feb. 20   Kuhn stages a large pro-Nazi rally in New York City's Madison Square Garden supposedly to celebrate George Washington's birthday.

Mar. 2   Kuhn is subpoenaed in New York on Bund tax evasion charges.

Mar. 4   Nazi Germany occupies the Czech lands of Bohemia and Moravia.

Apr. 6   US Attorney General Frank Murphy issues the FBI's 1937 investigation of the Bund.

May 27   Kuhn is arrested on charges of taking thousands of dollars from the Bund's treasury.

June 26   New Jersey legislature passes an amendment prohibiting production and dissemination of racial and religious hatred propaganda and to making it illegal for Bund members to appear in public in a uniform similar to the one of Nazi Germany.

July 4   Under Klapprott's direction, Nazi salutes and uniforms bearing the swastika are seen during the Independence Day celebration on camp grounds, in violation of state law.

July 6   New Jersey State Alcoholic Beverage Commission revokes Nordland's temporary liquor license.

July 12   Violation of New Jersey's June 26 amendment becomes a misdemeanor.

July 14   Andover authorities deny renewal of Nordland's liquor license on the grounds that Klapprott, who holds the license, violated the anti-uniform law.

Aug. 14   Diplomats representing Nazi Germany and the Soviet Union sign a non-aggression pact. War is imminent.

Sept. 1   Nazi Germany invades western Poland, sparking World War II.

Sept. 13   New Jersey State Alcoholic Beverage Commission upholds Andover Township's refusal to renew Camp Nordland's liquor license.

Sept. 17   The Soviet Union invades eastern Poland, in accordance with its agreement with Nazi Germany.

Nov. 4   The New Jersey Supreme Court refuses to review the State Alcohol Beverage Commission's decision against Nordland.

Dec. 5   Kuhn receives sentence up to five years in Sing Sing prison (Ossining, New York) for tax evasion and embezzlement.

                 Gerhard Wilhelm Kunze, born in Camden, New Jersey, steps in to replace Kuhn as leader of the German-American Bund.

1940

Jan. 3   The Dies Committee reports its finding about the Bund to Congress.

Apr. 9   Nazi Germany invades Norway and Denmark.

May 10   Nazi Germany invades the Netherlands and Belgium, quickly making its way to France.

July 4   Sussex County Sheriff Quick issues warrants to arrest Bund members at Camp Nordland for violation of the anti-uniform and hate laws. Klapprott is jailed for the night.

Aug. 18   A joint meeting of the Bund and the Ku Klux Klan takes place at Nordland.

Sept. 12   A huge explosion of the dynamite manufacturing at the Hercules Powder plant at Kenvil (near Nordland) occurs. The plant has been ramping up production for the US armed forces and allies.

Sept. 13   Sheriff Quick and assisting police raid Nordland. They seize stacks of antisemitic literature and a rifle with telescopic sight.

Sept. 16   President Franklin Delano Roosevelt signs the Selective Training and Service Act, requiring men between the ages of 21 and 36 to register with their local draft boards.

1941

Jan. 31   Nine officers of the Bund, including Kuhn's replacement and Klapprott, are sentenced to up to two years in state prison by the Sussex County Court of Common Pleas for racial hatred. Klapprott is also fined $2,000.

May 30	At the request of New Jersey attorney general David Wilentz and Sheriff Quick, a dozen local members of the American Legion raid and close Nordland. The Bund, to avoid losing the camp completely, transfers ownership to 217 individual Bund members just hours before the charter is revoked.
June 3	By unanimous vote, New Jersey state legislature repeals the charter of the German-American Bund Auxiliary, which owned Nordland and orders it to dispose of the property immediately.
June 10	Camp Nordland property is seized over the protests of the new owners.
Dec. 5	NJ Supreme Court finds the hate law in violation of Article I, Paragraph 5 of the state constitution and the 14th Amendment of the US Constitution. The court finds the Bund's ideas "revolting to any fairminded [*sic*] man" but not a danger to the state (State of NJ v. Klapprott, 127 NJL 395, 1941).
Dec. 7	Japanese military forces attack US naval ships at Pearl Harbor, Hawaii.
Dec. 8	The United States declares war on Japan.
Dec. 11	The United States declares war on Germany and Italy.
Dec. 14	The German-American Bund stages its last official act, a children's Christmas pageant in New York City.

SOURCE NOTES

PART I: FANFARE, 1937

"We've done nothing wrong"—"'Heils' Fade Away as Camp
Nordland Entertains 2,000," *The Morning Call* (Paterson, NJ),
July 26, 1937.

Southbury Says No—Harry Ferguson, "Connecticut Villagers Ban
Nazi Camp in Town Limits," *The Morning Call* (Paterson, NJ),
December 16, 1937.

PART II: PUSH AND PULL, 1938-1939

On the Way Home from Washington's Birthday Celebration—Warren
Grover, *Nazis in Newark* (New York: Routledge, 2017), 213.

"I am pleased . . . German-Austria."—Adolf Hitler before the
German parliament, February 20, 1938, "Neues Europa,"
der-fuehrer.org/reden/english/38-02-20.htm.

I Wonder—"Czechs Re-Assert Strong Opposition to Nazi Invasion,"
and "Goering Asserts Nazis May Extend European Control,"
Morning Call (Paterson, NJ), March 12, 1938.

Gold—"Big Guns Sent Up by Nazis," *Record* (Hackensack, NJ),
October 1, 1938.

More Germans in a Bigger Empire—"Hitler Gets Welcome by Half
Million," *Record* (Hackensack, NJ), October 1, 1938.

Germany Has Gone Crazy—"Nazis Smash, Loot and Burn Jewish Shops and Temples," *New York Times*, November 1, 1938.

At Madison Square Garden—"22,000 Nazis Hold Rally in Garden: Police Check Foes," *New York Times*, February 21, 1939.

The World's a Series of Punching Bags—Edward W. Beattie Jr., "Hacha Signs Pact for Rule by Nazis," *Morning Post* (Camden, NJ), March 15, 1939, and "Chamberlain to Keep to Course," *Record* (Hackensack, NJ), March 15, 1939.

Monkey in the Middle—"Reich and Soviet Agree on No-War Pact"— *Morning Press* (Camden, NJ), August 22, 1939.

War!—""Poland Bombed" and "Warsaw Calls for Britain's Aid," *Paterson* (NJ) *Evening News*, September 1, 1939.

PART III: THE DOOR CLOSES, 1940-1941

Colors of War—"The British beat back . . . Great Britain and China," *Herald-News* (Passaic, NJ), September 28, 1940.

BIBLIOGRAPHY

PRIMARY SOURCES

Federal Bureau of Investigation. "Fritz Julius Kuhn, Part 2 of 10."
FBI Records: The Vault. vault.fbi.gov/fritz-julius-kuhn/fritz-julius-kuhn-part-02-of/view.

———. "Fritz Julius Kuhn, Part 4 of 10." FBI Records: The Vault.
vault.fbi.gov/fritz-julius-kuhn/fritz-julius-kuhn-part-04-of-10/view.

———. "Fritz Julius Kuhn, Part 8 of 10." FBI Records: The Vault.
vault.fbi.gov/fritz-julius-kuhn/fritz-julius-kuhn-part-08-of-10/view.

———. "German-American Federation/Bund." FBI Records:
The Vault. vault.fbi.gov/german-american-bund.

Museum of Jewish Heritage. "Nazis on Long Island: The Story of
Camp Siegfried." YouTube, January 21, 2022. youtube.com/watch?v=UGJW1VQo1Ts.

Pete Green Productions. "NJ's Hitler Youth Camp, Camp Nordland!"
July 27, 2016. youtube.com/watch?v=GhO4MIRYemU.

US Congress. *Congressional Record*. 75th Cong., 1st session, 1937.
Vol. 81, pt. 6.

———. *Congressional Record*. 75th Cong., 1st session, 1937.
Vol. 81, pt. 7.

———. *Congressional Record*. 75th Cong., 3rd session, 1938. Vol. 83, pt. 2.

———. *Congressional Record*. 75th Cong., 3rd session, 1938. Vol. 83, pt. 3.

———. *Congressional Record*. 75th Cong., 3rd session, 1938. Vol. 83, pt. 7.

———. *Congressional Record*. 76th Cong., 3rd session, 1940. Vol. 86, pt. 6.

———. *Investigation of Un-American Propaganda Activities in the United States: Special Committee on Un-American Activities, House of Representatives, Seventy-Seventh Congress, First Session on H. Res. 282; Appendix; German-American Bund*. London: Forgotten Books, 2018.

US National Archives. "German-American Bund Rally Address by Its Leader Fritz Kuhn." Madison Square Garden, New York City, February 20, 1939. youtube.com/watch?v=_nLk3uwZy5M.

———. *Volks-Deutsche Jungen in USA*, (Ethnic German Youth in USA), August 1, 2014. youtube.com/watch?v=JxJ4TV1UtqU.

BOOKS AND JOURNAL ARTICLES

Bell, Leland Virgil. "Anatomy of a Hate Movement: The German American Bund, 1936–1941." PhD diss. University of West Virginia, 1968.

———. *In Hitler's Shadow: The Anatomy of American Nazism*. Port Washington, New York: Kennikat Press, 1973.

Bernstein, Arnie. *Swastika Nation: Fritz Kuhn and the Rise and Fall of the German-American Bund*. New York: St. Martin's Press, 2013.

Canedy, Susan. *America's Nazis: A Democratic Dilemma, A History of the German American Bund*. Menlo Park, CA: Markgraf Publications Group, 1990.

Cunningham, John T. *Newark*. Newark: New Jersey Historical Society, 1966.

DeJong, Louis. *The German Fifth Column in the Second World War*. Chicago: University of Chicago Press, 1956.

Diamond, Sander A. *The Nazi Movement in the United States, 1924–1941*. Ithaca, NY: Cornell University Press, 1974.

Dies, Martin. *The Trojan Horse in America*. New York: Dodd, Mead and Co., 1940.

Federal Writers' Project of the Works Progress Administration for the State of New Jersey. *The WPA Guide to 1930s New Jersey*. New Brunswick: Rutgers University Press, 1986.

Glaser, Martha. "The German-American Bund in New Jersey." *New Jersey History* 92, no. 1 (1974): 33–49.

Grover, Warren. *Nazis in Newark*. New York: Routledge, 2017.

Hart, Bradley W. *Hitler's American Friends: The Third Reich's Supporters in the United States*. New York: St. Martin's Press/ Thomas Dunne Books, 2018.

Helmreich, William B. *The Enduring Community: The Jews of Newark and MetroWest*. New Brunswick, NJ: Transaction, 1999.

Remak, Joachim. "Friends of the New Germany: The Bund and German-American Relations." *Journal of Modern History* 29, no. 1 (March 1957): 38–41.

NEWSPAPER ARTICLES

"3 Bund Leaders Seized in Jersey for Anti-Uniform Law Violation." *New York Times*, July 5, 1940.

"2,000 Rout Kuhn in Rock Barrage at Hudson Hall." *Record* (Hackensack, NJ), October 30, 1938.

"12,000 at Nazi Fete Hear Boycott Plan." *New York Times*, September 6, 1937.

"22,000 Nazis Hold Rally in Garden." *New York Times*, February 21, 1939.

Beattie, Edward W., Jr. "Hacha Signs Pact for Rule by Nazis." *Morning Post* (Camden, NJ), March 15, 1939.

"Big Guns Sent Up by Nazis," *The Record* (Hackensack, NJ), October 1, 1938.

Brackett, Milton. "Southbury Zoning Barring Nazi Camp." *New York Times*, December 15, 1937.

"Britain and France Send Ultimatums." *New York Times,* September 2, 1939.

"Bund Camp Reopens." *Courier News* (Bridgewater, NJ), May 2, 1938.

"Bund Camp Under Fire." *New York Times*, November 5, 1939.

"Bund Chief, 8 Others Jailed in New Jersey for Race Hatred Talks at Camp Nordland." *New York Times*, February 1, 1941.

"[B]und Liquor Sale Barred by Jersey." *New York Times*, September 14, 1939.

"Bund's Defiance Arouses Jersey." *New York Times*, July 6, 1939.

"Burnett Revokes Camp Nordland Liquor License." *Morning Call* (Paterson, NJ), July 7, 1939.

Caldwell, William A. "Simeon Stylites." *Bergen Evening Record* (Hackensack, NJ), August 23, 1940.

"Chamberlain to Keep to Course." *Record* (Hackensack, NJ), March 15, 1939.

"Czechs Re-Assert Strong Opposition to Nazi Invasion." *Morning Call* (Paterson, NJ), March 12, 1938.

"Dickstein Lists 46 Nazi Agitators." *New York Times*, July 28, 1937.

"Dickstein Lists More 'Nazi Aides.'" *New York Times*, August 5, 1937.

"Dies Investigator in Blast Inquiry." *New York Times*, September 16, 1940.

Ferguson, Harry. "Connecticut Villagers Ban Nazi Camp in Town Limits." *Morning Call* (Paterson, NJ), December 16, 1937.

"France Mobilizes; 8,000,000 on Call." *New York Times*, September 2, 1939.

"'Gentile-Ruled U.S.' Is Program of Bund." *New York Times*, September 5, 1938.

"German Army Attacks Poland—Cities Bombed—British Mobilizing." *New York Times*, September 1, 1939.

"German Camp Defended." *New York Times*, August 2, 1937.

"Germans Occupy Denmark, Attack Oslo; Norway Then Joins Against Hitler; Capital Is Reported Bombed from Air." *New York Times*, April 9, 1940.

"Goering Asserts Nazis May Extend European Control." *Morning Call* (Paterson, NJ), March 12, 1938.

"Hague Fete Bars Nazis." *New York Times*, June 6, 1938.

"'Heil's Fade Away as Camp Nordland Entertains 2,000." *Morning Call* (Paterson, NJ), July 26, 1937.

"Hitler Demands Full French Surrender." *New York Times*, June 22, 1940.

"Hitler Gets Welcome by Half Million." *Record* (Hackensack, NJ), October 1, 1938.

"Immorality at Yaphank Bund Camp Bared by Brooklyn Girl at Dies Quiz." *Brooklyn Daily Eagle*, August 18, 1939.

"The International Situation." *New York Times*, April 9, 1940.

"Jersey Bars Sale of Liquor by Bund." *New York Times*, July 15, 1939.

"Jersey Bund Loses Its Liquor Permit." *New York Times*, July 7, 1939.

"Jersey Veterans Rout Nazi Leader." *New York Times*, October 3, 1938.

"Jews Blamed by Miss Meade." *Bergen Evening Record* (Hackensack, NJ), October 11, 1938.

"Klan Has 'Americanism' Rally at Bund Camp; Members of Both Orders Mingle in Jersey." *New York Times*, August 19, 1940.

"Kuhn Cheered in Jersey." *New York Times*, October 3, 1938.

"Kuhn Found Guilty on All Five Counts; He Faces 30 Years." *New York Times*, November 30, 1939.

"London Threatens—Sends Final Demand to Germany to Cease Her Attack on Poland." *New York Times*, September 2, 1939.

"Nazi Camp Head Scoffs at Charge." *Central New Jersey Home News* (New Brunswick, NJ), September 9, 1937.

"Nazi Camp Invites Untermyer to Visit." *New York Times*, September 27, 1937.

"Nazi Putsch Here Is Quickly Denied." *New York Times*, September 10, 1937.

"Nazi-Soviet Pact Alarms World." *Courier News* (Bridgewater, NJ), August 22, 1939.

"Nazis Invade Holland, Belgium, Luxembourg by Land and Air." *New York Times*, May 10, 1940.

"Nazis Open Sussex Camp." *New York Times*, July 19, 1937.

"Nazis Smash, Loot and Burn Jewish Shops and Temples." *New York Times*, November 1, 1938.

"Pact Warns Russia Too, Nazis Say." *Herald-News* (Passaic, NJ), September 28, 1940.

"Poland Bombed." *Paterson Evening News*, September 1, 1939.

"Protest Planned at German Camp." *New York Times*, August 9, 1937.

"Reich and Soviet Army Agree on No-War Pact." *Morning Press* (Camden, NJ), August 22, 1939.

"Roosevelt Pledge—He Promises Efforts to Keep the U.S. Out of War." *New York Times*, September 2, 1939.

"Says New Jersey Is Nazi 'Hotbed.'" *Daily Home News* (New Brunswick, NJ), August 12, 1937.

"Township Sets Up $500 Shooting Gallery Fee Aimed at Jersey Bund's Camp Nordland." *New York Times*, July 1, 1938.

"Veterans Ask Inquiries." *New York Times*, July 27, 1937.

"Veterans to Watch Bund Camp." *New York Times*, June 5, 1938.

Warsaw Calls for Britain's Aid." *Paterson Evening News*, September 1, 1939.

"Wilentz Advises Nazi Question Outside Offices." *Courier News* (Bridgewater, NJ), August 6, 1937.

FOR FURTHER READING/VIEWING

Burns, Ken, Lynn Novick, and Sarah Botstein. *The U.S. and the Holocaust. American Experience*, 2022. pbs.org/kenburns/us-and-the-holocaust/.

Chee, Traci. *We Are Not Free*. New York: Houghton Mifflin Harcourt, 2020.

Engle, Margarita. *Tropical Secrets: Holocaust Refugees in Cuba.* New York: Henry Holt, 2009.

Roth, Philip. *The Plot Against America*. New York: Houghton Mifflin, 2004.

Voigt Kaplan, Jennifer. *Crushing of the Red Flowers*. New York: Ig Publishing, 2019.

Wilson, Kip. *White Rose*. New York: Versify/Houghton Mifflin Harcourt, 2019.

PICTURE CREDITS

Getty Images: 337, 338.
Steve Arnold: 339.